CAUGHT

Lolita London

Copyright © 2016 by Lolita London

All rights reserved. No part of this publication may be reproduced, distributed, or transmitted in any form or by any means, including photocopying, recording, or other electronic or mechanical methods, without the prior written permission of the publisher, except in the case of brief quotations embodied in critical reviews and certain other noncommercial uses permitted by copyright law.

Table of Contents

Chapter 1 1

Chapter 2 21

Chapter 3 42

Chapter 4 51

Chapter 5 77

Chapter 6 85

Chapter 7 112

Chapter 8 126

Chapter 9 145

Chapter 10 164

Chapter 11 174

Chapter 12 206

Chapter 13 215

Chapter 14 228

Epilogue 258

Chapter 1

The door of The Teahouse brothel swung wide open to let a strong gust of wind blast through the opening, and Maggie Green narrowed her eyes to watch which piece of humanity would be blown inside by it.

"Will I service this one?" Samantha asked.

Maggie ignored the coarse voice of the skinny girl standing close by as a slight smirk flashed across her face. The man that stepped across the threshold and slammed the door shut was wrapped up against the cold of a brisk autumn afternoon. The large scarf around his neck was hauled up to cover his mouth, while the almost oversize cap on his head cast a shadow over his face. It disguised some of his recognizable features well, but the hulking, muscular physique was something that no amount of clothing could hide.

It revealed his identity to Maggie, and it wasn't the cold of the day that sent a shiver trickling down her spine. The flicker of anticipation was instant at the appearance of Thomas Winterbourne, and she knew there was only one reason he was there.
"Did you hear me?" Samantha queried.

Maggie turned her attention from the approaching man to look at the pretty face of the skinny girl.

"I heard you, dear," she answered.

"And... do you..."

"No," Maggie interrupted. "You run along and make yourself some tea. I'll deal with this gentleman."

Gentleman was the correct term for the man she returned her gaze to. The majority of customers that frequented the brothel were rough-looking, ill-mannered and uneducated. That certainly wasn't true of Thomas Winterbourne. He might very well have the physique of a common dockworker, but his wealthy, refined and educated upbringing led him to be trained as a doctor and Maggie was all too aware of this fact. Her gaze fixed on the way he carefully removed the gloves he was wearing and the slender, long-fingered, well-manicured hands were another giveaway sign of his identity. They reached up to pull the scarf down, but it was Maggie that spoke first.

"Spent your morning with a patient, Mr. Winterbourne?" she asked quietly.

It was a question she already knew the answer to before Thomas nodded his head. He was heir to a significant family fortune that would come his way on the death of his elderly parents, and the money he already received was enough to see him live a comfortable life in a large west end mansion. That allowed him to concentrate his efforts on researching and writing about his area of specialty, but Maggie knew that he would see patients that were referred to him by friends and family.

The ladies that arrived at his home were looking for a treatment to cure female hysteria or, as Maggie called it, night terrors. Thomas Winterbourne's approach to this was something that she was all too aware of and why she smirked when he first walked in the door. His patients were likely shocked at the massaging of their naked bodies that he assured them would deal with the problem. However, their desire for a cure, as well as the professional qualifications and the standing in the community of the doctor suggesting the unconventional treatment, convinced them to go along with it.

Maggie knew for sure that it wasn't only for the benefit of the patients though. While Thomas genuinely believed that his methods would heal the ladies referred to him, there was also the not insignificant matter of his own sexual proclivities. That administering the treatment got him so erect and turned on was a source of humiliation for him but also something that he was unable to control. He considered the pleasure he took from it as grotesquely perverse, and that made him question if his own nature was the same.

It left him unmarried at the age of 28, since he couldn't bring himself to inflict the shamefulness of his secret desires on a wife. He'd desperately searched for a more conventional method of getting himself aroused, but nothing compared with the pure adrenaline rush of having a woman naked on his examination table and completely under his control. The main problem with this was that he lacked an outlet for his lust at home.

The refined ladies that were his patients dressed and exited the examination room as soon as the treatment ended, which left him ashamed and frustrated. That was the reason for his visits to a house of ill repute in an area far enough from his mansion that he was sure he wouldn't be caught doing it. The state of rampant sexual arousal that he was left in after dealing with a patient needed relieving, and it was with a working girl at The Teahouse brothel that he got this.

Her position as the Madame at the establishment meant that Maggie was generally there when he made an appearance, and that gave her the chance to take advantage of it. At 32, she couldn't compete with the younger, slimmer, prettier girls that made their living in the place, but her attributes seemed to be appreciated by Thomas at least. He didn't complain that she was usually the woman on the receiving end of one of his medical massages in the brothel, and she was more than happy to give him the relief he needed at the end of it.

"Mrs. Harper," she shouted.

Seconds later, an old lady came out of a room at the back of the place and the slightly annoyed expression on her face was all too obvious.

"What?" she asked.

"Watch the place until I get back," Maggie went on. She then looked at the man that was now her customer. "It's the same room as always."

Thomas simply nodded his head and waited for her to step past him before following on. They made their way through a door to a hallway and walked to the set of steps at the end of it. Maggie wondered if the man behind her was staring at her ample behind as she climbed to the first floor then led the way along to a door. She held it open for him to walk through then followed. The click of the lock trapped them inside and gave them the privacy they needed.

Thomas was already removing his coat, cap and scarf to hang them on a hook in the wall when she turned, and it fully revealed his features. His thin face was tight lipped, and baring his head allowed the unruly, curly, dark red hair to spill across his forehead. He used his fingers to comb it to the side, but it still looked untidy when he finished. Watching what he was doing made Maggie raise a hand to her own red hair, although her color came courtesy of a bottle rather than being natural. She fussed with the combs and pins holding her somewhat garish tresses piled high on her head as she walked across the room.

"Do you want the usual, Mr. Winterbourne?" she asked.

"Yes," he replied.

It was the first word out of his mouth since he arrived at the place and the deep, rumbling baritone of his voice brought the smirk back to Maggie's face. She was already breathing a bit heavier at the prospect of what was about take place and couldn't stop her sense of anticipation growing. She stopped in front of a shabby wooden cabinet and opened the door. It was the only piece of furniture in the room apart from the single bed and it held the equipment she needed. The four pieces of rope she picked from a shelf were long, with each ending in a small noose.

Maggie's hands were shaking as she closed the cabinet doors and turned to walk across to the bed. She dropped the pieces of rope on the mattress and saw Thomas staring at her. He got out his wallet when he moved closer, and she accepted the coins that he held out then put them in her pocket.

"Not counting them?" he asked.

"I trust you," Maggie said with a grin.

She was aware of his unwavering gaze on her as she began to strip. Her clothing was as outrageously colored as her hair and covered a voluptuous figure that was now running to more rounded than she really wanted. She removed the bright blue shawl from around her shoulders and it revealed a deep cleavage that the tight purple blouse she was wearing struggled to contain. The top few buttons were already loosened and she knew that it gave Thomas a glimpse of her ample bosom. As she undid more, she revealed skin that was pale white and perfumed.

Maggie dropped the blouse on top of the shawl, but left her bra in place. Her hands went to the buttons at her hip and she loosened them to let the billowing dark skirt slide down her thick legs and pool around her feet. She kicked it away and removed her shoes before stepping closer the bed.

"Which way to start?" she asked.

"Face down please," Thomas said.

She could already hear the tinge of excitement in his voice and it matched her own. There was no doubt the kinky game of her playing a patient to receive one of his medical massages was a turn on for him. Her enjoyment of it was why she always made sure she was the one to receive it when Thomas made a visit to the brothel. She could tell he was somewhat ashamed of his desires and wished he could suppress them, but that wasn't a problem that afflicted her. The touch of his slender fingers was something she craved when she was alone in the room with him, and she eagerly dropped face down on the bed.

She shuddered at the grip on her naked leg and knew what was coming. The noose of one of the ropes was slipped around her ankle and it tightened in place as the other end was tied to the post at the bottom of the bed. When her other ankle was grabbed to secure it in place, it left her legs spread wide open, with only her bloomers protecting her modesty. It wouldn't be long before that ended and her pulse was racing as Thomas slipped the noose of another rope around her right wrist. Her arm was stretched out as the rope was knotted to a bedpost, and when the job of tying her down was completed, she was left completely at the mercy of the man standing over her.

"So tell me your symptoms," he said as his long manicured fingers touched on the pale skin of her neck.

Maggie played out the game he liked and pretended to be a patient in need of help. It was the same words she always used, but he didn't seem to mind.

"In the dead of night my mind conjures up terrible images, doctor," she said. "It leaves me shaking, sweating and unable to control my limbs."

"Does it start when you are sleeping or awake?" he went on.

"Awake," Maggie said.

The massaging touch of his fingers kneading her shoulders was both relaxing and arousing. She was all too aware of the slickness that began to stain her bloomers almost straight away and shudders afflicted her body as the light touch of his fingers slid down her spine. Thomas released her bra and she knew her large breasts would spill free when she was turned over. That was yet to come and she tensed as his fingers slid lower still. They caressed and groped her buttocks through her bloomers and she closed her eyes tightly.

"Does this help?" he asked.

"Yes, doctor," she said in a hoarse voice.

Her exhilaration was on the rise and it surged to more as his touch slid between her thighs. She was aware of his gasp when he felt the wetness on the silky material. His fingers sought out her swollen pussy lips and stroked along them.

"We need to get your panties out of the way for the treatment to be successful," Thomas said.

"Yes, doctor," Maggie repeated.

The throb of his rampant erection made it strain against his underwear, and the racing beat of his heart brought out gasping breaths. He reached for the waistband of the bloomers and his gaze settled on Maggie's fleshy buttocks as he exposed them to his gaze. She gasped as he fondled and groped them before his slender fingers slipped back between her thighs. The ropes around her wrists and ankles chafed her skin as she writhed in pleasure. There was now nothing stopping Thomas's fingers stroking on her naked skin and the tension gripped her body.

"We need to make you lose yourself," he said. "It will cure you of your hysteria."

It was happening already as Maggie gave herself over to the sensual delight of the soft caresses along her pussy lips. The treatment was blatantly sexual, and she wondered if it was what he did to his real patients or whether the fact that he was in a brothel and paying for the services of a girl allowed him to take his fantasies further. In truth she didn't particularly care one way or the other as her body responded to the rougher stroking between her thighs. It easily spread her swollen lips apart and her muscles tightened as the slight penetration dipped inside her.

She was anxious for more as she squirmed, but Thomas's fingers slid back out almost as soon as they entered her and she let out a quiet groan. The ropes holding her wrists in place were loosened and a gentle touch stroked along her spine then right down the back of her right leg to her ankle. The rope was released and then the one holding her left leg in place was as well. She waited as the bloomers were dragged down and off before rolling over.

A glance at the doctor showed the huge bulge already showing at his crotch. The act of tying her down and using her body as if he was administering a treatment was bringing him fully erect and her gaze remained on it. The game wasn't over yet. Not by a long way, and she was hurriedly tied down to the bed again. It stretched her out on her back with her legs spread wide apart. The bra cups were dragged from her breasts to expose them, but Thomas ignored her impressive curves as his long fingers kneaded her shoulders again.

She caught his gaze and saw the intense animal lust that was overcoming him. It was apparent that no matter how much he tried to suppress his perversions, he was unable to do it. His breath came out in short, sharp gasps as his gaze moved lower and his hands followed it. Maggie began to squirm again as her tits were groped with an almost obsessive passion. The rough touch of fingers sinking deep in her soft flesh made her groan and the doctor nodded his head.

"Louder," he urged her. "It helps with your cure."

Maggie let out a despairing groan that was only partly faked as the delight of the touch on her breasts rippled down her body and between her thighs. The burst of tingling heat made her ass lift up from the bed and the ropes chafed her naked skin again as she strained and struggled against them. Not that she wanted to be released. She was being teased and toyed to an orgasm that she wanted more and more with each passing second. She knew it wouldn't be long in coming when Thomas's fingers slid lower on her body. They caressed over her belly and she willed them to speed up. The game of a pretend medical therapy carried on and she wanted to beg for a touch between her thighs, but she did no more than keep groaning.

"This is how to rid yourself of your symptoms," Thomas said when his fingers slid to slick skin.

Maggie clenched her buttocks as her body arched up, and she grimaced at the uncomfortable pain of the ropes grazing on her pale skin. Her breathing was shallow and ragged as Thomas's fingers stroked along her slick, swollen lips. When they dipped inside her pussy this time, they stayed inside and the swell of ecstasy began to burn out of control as she was made to take their full length.

Thomas's free hand found her clit and he began to punish the erect bud with rough strokes. Maggie really was losing her mind as she gave herself over to the pure delight of what was taking place.

"Yes… yes, it's working," Thomas said as he started to finger her.

He kept the pressure on Maggie's clitoris with circling strokes as he fucked touches in and out of her slick cunt until she was writhing around as if she was in agony. It was a deeply pleasurable torment she was in the grip of, however, as her body responded to the sensual onslaught. Thomas leaned his head closer to watch as he drove his fingers in wet pussy with increasingly forceful strokes that gave his patient her medicine.

It all became too much for Maggie as she was taken to an orgasm. The tightening of her muscles made her body arch up and it was a sign she recognized. Suddenly there was no stopping herself being tipped over the edge to fall into a climax. It quickly overwhelmed her as the rippling shudders wracked her body and her neck stretched out as she pressed her head back against the mattress. There was no need to fake a groan now as her cries rang out. Thomas plunged his fingers deep to let her quivering pussy walls ripple around the stiff penetration until the convulsing spasms slowly began to fade from her body.

"All better now," he said.

Maggie slumped to the bed and gasped for breath. She glanced to see how big the bulge was in Thomas's pants now and knew that the game wasn't over yet. The ropes were loosened from her wrists and it allowed her to sit up.

"Are you ready for your relief, doctor?" she said.

"Yes," he replied and she heard the slight shame that came through in his voice.

He couldn't contain his lust at having a woman tied down for his use and had confessed to her on a number of occasions that it was the same when he was actually treating a patient. It seemed perverse and somehow degrading that an intellectual man such as himself was a slave to his baser instincts, but there was no controlling it. He looked down as Maggie opened the buttons at his crotch and slipped her hand through the gap. She wrapped her fingers around a rampant erection that throbbed in her hand as she pulled it out.

Thomas groaned as she stroked along his full length. His breath rasped out and his legs trembled as the tingling pressure in his balls grew stronger second by second until he was lost to the pleasure wracking his body. Maggie slid her free hand through the gap in his pants to cup her fingers around his balls and massaged them as she continued stroking along his erection. She looked up to see his eyes tightly shut and his face contorted as he gave up the struggle to hold back. He put his hands on his hips and leaned back to push his crotch forward as the pure bliss of the touches on his erection brought on the release.

Maggie anticipated it and quickened the motion of her hand to make her customer completely lose control. Her eyes lit up as she watched the long string of cum shoot from the tip. There was no getting out of the way and it splashed across her breasts. The first eruption of thick white was followed by more as Thomas's lust spilled out all over her chest. The jerking thrusts of his hips died away as his ardor finally cooled and he let out a gasp as he stepped back to look at what he'd done.

"I must apologize for…" he started.

"You paid your money," Maggie interrupted him.

He simply nodded his head, but she could see the embarrassment on his face as the arousal drained away to leave his mind clear again.

"Let me loose, will you?" she said.

Thomas stuffed his softening erection back in his pants then stepped forward to free her ankles from the bonds holding them to the bed. He then busied himself straightening his clothes while she got up. She used the shawl to clean the stickiness from her chest before quickly putting her clothes back on.

"Thank you," Thomas said, but his gaze remained on the floor and he didn't look at her.

"You're welcome, dear," Maggie replied. "You come back whenever you want."

He simply nodded his head then moved to the hook on the wall to put his coat, cap and scarf back on.

"Going home now?" she asked when she approached him.

Thomas finished what he was doing then shook his head.

"I have some business to attend to first," he said.

"Not having problems, I hope," Maggie went on as she opened the door for him.

"No, nothing serious," he replied as they walked along the hallway back to the stairs. "One of my housemaids needed to leave, so I need to arrange for a replacement."

Maggie's ears pricked up at the news.

"I hope you find them from a reputable place," she said. "You want to make sure you get a trustworthy girl that will do a good job."

"The Colwell Agency," he replied. "It's the one I've always used and I've never suffered any problems with the maids they supply."

A smile spread across Maggie's face, but she said no more as they walked the rest of the way to the exit.

"Have a good night," she said when she opened the door to let him leave.

She watched him disappear into the darkness and suspected that his carriage was parked on a nearby street.

"Can I go back to my room?" Mrs. Harper said.

Maggie turned to look at the elderly woman and shook her head.

"I need to go out for a while, but I shouldn't be long," she said.

The curse of Mrs. Harper was quiet, but Maggie ignored it as she got her coat and put it on. When she left the building, she turned up her collar against the cold and hurried through the dark streets. It was almost six in the evening and she wondered what time the Colwell Agency closed. There was only one way to find out and she quickened her pace to get there. The sight of the large carriage sitting in front of the agency building stopped her in her tracks and she kept out of sight as she watched. Ten minutes later, she saw Thomas Winterbourne walk out. She waited until his carriage disappeared from view before making a move.

The manager of the Colwell Agency was known to her and she was aware of just what he enjoyed on his visits to The Teahouse brothel. She suspected his wife wouldn't be too happy with it, and that gave her some leverage to get what it was she wanted from him. When she waked in the door of the building, she stepped over to the small reception desk straight away.

"I'd like to see Mr. Hollinger," she said.

The woman behind the desk narrowed her eyes as she stared.

"Who shall I say is calling?"

"Maggie Green," she replied and watched as the woman got up and walked over to a door.

Maggie was sure that some gentle persuasion would get her what she needed. In truth she would never dream of telling a customer's wife what they got up to in the brothel... but Mr. Hollinger didn't know that. She smiled as the receptionist came out of the room and beckoned her over.

"You can go right in."

She did just that and closed the door behind her.

"What the hell are you doing here?" Mr. Hollinger hissed and she saw the concerned expression on his face.

"Don't worry," Maggie assured him and smiled. "All I need is a small favor and I'm sure you'll be more than willing to help me."

Chapter 2

The loping strides of Andy Kent covered the ground easily and Jenny struggled to keep up with him. She wanted to yell at him to slow down, but knew it would annoy the man she considered her mentor. He'd spent more than ten years teaching her to blend in to the background, to not stand out, to be as invisible as possible to those around. It helped in the line of business they pursued, and she was all too aware that a shout would bring attention to them and definitely wouldn't fit in with those rules.

She tried to stride out to catch up, but her petite size meant that her shorter legs didn't cover the ground nearly as quickly since Andy seemed intent on getting wherever he was taking her as fast as humanly possible. Where that was, she didn't know, although it was a world away from their usual surroundings. The densely populated tenement streets they normally frequented disappeared from view almost thirty minutes ago, and Jenny wasn't sure she fit in the salubrious surroundings they were now passing through.

The buildings were no longer tenements and the large mansion-like properties were getting bigger. The streets were also a lot quieter and the few men and women they did pass were smartly dressed. It made her look down at the shabby clothes she was wearing and they certainly didn't match up to the elegant outfits of the people she saw.

"So much for blending in," she muttered.

It was the same for Andy; the worn hem of the scruffy dark cape he liked to wear over a dark suit was all too apparent as it fluttered in the wind. He seemed unconcerned by this as he continued to move confidently towards their destination, and when he stopped at a crossroads, Jenny wondered if they were there. She let out a sigh of relief as she finally caught up to him.

"What are we…" she started, but his hand shot up to stop her words.

"Don't speak," Andy admonished her in a quiet voice. "You're interrupting me."

An indignant expression crossed Jenny's face as the slight irritation welled up.

"What do you…" she let out, but she was cut off again before she finished her sentence.

"You're doing it again," Andy snapped. "Be quiet."

He looked around as if he was trying to decide which way to go and Jenny realized they hadn't arrived at their destination yet. Her mouth opened to speak again, but the forty-year-old man was already on the move before she said anything, and his loping strides quickly put distance between them. She cursed quietly as she started walking again to follow and cast her gaze around. The people that occupied the properties they were passing were obviously wealthy and the world they lived in was something that she could only imagine.

It was a million miles away from her own upbringing, with Andy being as near to a father as she ever had. He wasn't though, and in truth she didn't actually know who her real father was. It was a question she asked constantly when she was a little girl, but her mother passed away when Jenny was eight without ever giving an answer. It always seemed strange that the information was kept from her, but the death of the only parent she ever knew meant there was little she could do about it.

She grew accustomed to poverty during the early years of her life, but it was nothing compared to the destitution she endured in the orphanage she was sent to following her mother's death. It was a place she quickly grew to loathe with a vengeance. The daily punishments were handed out for the most trivial of reasons, with the religious zeal of the aristocratic owners meaning that almost everything she and the other children did was a sin that needed to be beaten out of them. It gave her a hatred of the upper classes that burned in her.

Jenny lasted a year in the place before deciding that life on the streets would be a better alternative. She quickly found out she was mistaken and that a nine-year-old child was an easy target for the bullies, drunkards and other lowlifes that preyed on them. This was especially true for girls, and it almost got her in serious trouble when she was cornered by an older man intent on satisfying his lust on her. It was Andy that saved her from that terrible fate and gave her a life to look forward to.

As she followed in his wake that night, she wondered if she was going to be breaking in to one of the large properties they were passing. When she saw Andy come to a stop again, she was quick to catch up to him.

"What are we doing here?' she asked and managed to get the whole question out without Andy telling her to be quiet.

It didn't actually mean he would answer; instead he drew her into the dark shadow of the wall they were standing beside. The silence stretched out until it was unbearable for her and she couldn't stop herself asking the question again.

"Andy, what are…?"

Her irritation welled up when he interrupted her.

"What do you think of that place?" he asked and pointed across the street to a huge set of gates.

"Why, are you thinking of buying it?" Jenny let out sarcastically. The lightning quick slap of Andy's hand clipped the back of her head and she made a face as she rubbed it. "Alright, alright, there's no need for that," she complained as she turned to look at the property.

"So… what do you think?" he asked again.

Jenny shrugged her shoulders.

"It's massive, luxurious and probably filled with things we could sell for a lot of money," she commented.

Andy nodded his head but said nothing as he rubbed his chin and stared across the street. Jenny waited for him to say something more. He didn't and as the silence stretched out, she was compelled to fill it.

"Are you thinking about robbing the place?" she asked.

"In a manner of speaking," he replied.

Jenny narrowed her eyes as she turned to stare at him. His hat was pulled down low to obscure his face and she could barely make it out in the dark shadows they were standing in.

"Is there any chance you might actually tell me what's going on?" she let out. "Maybe in plain English and not riddles, so I understand what you're talking about."

"Maggie came up with an idea," Andy said.

The image of the redheaded, voluptuous, older woman sprang into Jenny's mind. It was usually Andy that devised the schemes and robberies his gang of thieves undertook, so she guessed that whatever Maggie came up with must be good if he was interested in it.

"She came up with an idea to do what exactly?" Jenny encouraged him.

""To get inside that property," Andy replied.

"Is that why we're here?" she went on.

"Yes," he told her. "But we're not going to do anything tonight. I just wanted to show you the place."

"Umm... OK," Jenny let out hesitantly. "And now that I've seen it, what am I supposed to do?"

The darkness didn't obscure the wide smile that spread across Andy's face as he looked directly at her.

"You go to the Colwell Agency tomorrow," he told her.

"I do what?" she let out in a surprised voice. "And why the hell would I do that?"

"Because that's the way we're going to get a girl in that property," Andy said as he pointed at it.

"Huh?" she let out in a confused voice.

"The owner of the place goes by the name of Thomas Winterbourne," Andy told her. "A doctor, according to Maggie, but more importantly for us a visitor to the fine establishment she is the Madame in."

"The man that lives in that huge house goes to an east end brothel?" Jenny let out in an astonished voice.

"Yes, and while he was there he let slip that he is in the market for a new maid," Andy went on. "Maggie found out that he uses the Colwell Agency to provide him with his household staff, and just by coincidence the owner of that business also frequents the brothel."

"So Maggie was able to call in a favor," Jenny said as she began to understand what was going on.

"Exactly," Andy said. "She put the offer to the owner that his wife would remain ignorant of his visits to a house of ill repute, as long as we get to supply the maid for that fine house."

"So we put someone we know in there to case it and the other residences in the neighborhood then steal what we can," Jenny said. "That's brilliant."

"That's what I thought when Maggie put the idea to me," he said. "And we both agree that you would make a perfect maid."

"Wait… what?" Jenny spluttered. "You want me to do it?"

"You're…" Andy started.

"No way!" Jenny exclaimed. "I'm not going to be a slave for some entitled, west end snob that thinks I'm a piece of dirt to be trodden on. Don't you remember all I told you about the orphanage I was in? I'm not putting myself in that position again."

She turned as if she was going to walk away, but Andy grabbed her hand.

"It won't be like the orphanage," he said. "You'll simply be working in his household and from what Maggie told me, Thomas Winterbourne is no upper class monster that looks down on others."

"They're all the same," Jenny spat out.

"Look, you're going in there as a thief, not a maid," Andy went on. "You check the place out and let us know what there is to steal. Being there will give you the chance to check out neighboring properties, and if you see an opportunity, you can rob them first. You then steal what you can from Thomas Winterbourne and get out of the place. If you loathe the upper class people as much as you say, this is a good chance to get back at them."

Jenny let out a sigh.

"I don't know," she said.

"You're the perfect person for it," Andy told her. "It might not look it in the clothes you normally wear, but you are a girl, and at nineteen years old you are the right age. I also need someone in there that is smart and I can trust. It has to be you."

"But if I do this the people in that house will know my face," Jenny protested. "That means there is a greater chance I'll be caught if suspicion falls on me once it's all over."

"We'll get Maggie to make you look like the pretty girl you are," Andy said and laughed. "Once it's over you can go back to your usual appearance. I would suspect the difference between the two is night and day and nobody will be any the wiser that the pretty maid that left is the scruffy tomboy that you normally are."

"But…" Jenny started but didn't get the chance to finish when she was interrupted.

"As well as that," Andy went on, "Thomas Winterbourne and Mr. Hollinger at the Colwell Agency are hardly likely to want it broadcast that they are using the services of a brothel. They might just accept what's happened and move on with their lives without saying anything."

Jenny was silent as she thought about it. The prospect of relieving some aristocratic families of their belongings did appeal, and she found herself coming round to the idea.

"Come on," urged Andy. "I need you for this, and think of the money we can make. This one job will set us up for a while."

The obligation she felt to him was there in her mind and she could see the eagerness in his eyes as his face came closer. He seemed excited by the prospect of what the clever scheme might bring them, and she finally agreed.

"OK, I'll do it," Jenny said.

"I knew you would," Andy said and engulfed her in a bear hug.

It revealed the softer side of the man that most people didn't see but Jenny knew was there. She'd been around him long enough to figure out that the hard-hearted personality he showed to the world wasn't the whole truth when it came to Andy Kent. The thieves he controlled stole not just for the benefit of him and the gang he led but also to help many of the waifs and strays in their neighborhood have a better life.

After saving her from the man that attacked her when she was nine years old, he seemed to recognize something in her that would make her an asset to his gang. Jenny took to a life of crime like a duck to water and rapidly became an expert at what she did. Her small size allowed her to get into places others couldn't and her quick brain gave her a smart enough mouth to talk herself out of most situations.

That didn't make her perfect at the job by any means, but the couple of instances when she ended up in court showed her why Andy relied so heavily on women and children. The judges tended to be much more lenient towards them, and the slap on the wrist she received on both occasions she stood in the dock was never going to turn her away from a life of crime.

It led her to where she was standing that night, with Andy suddenly realizing what he was doing and backing off. She could see his unease at unwittingly showing his softer side with the hug and the smile spread across her face.

"What are you smiling at?" he said in a gruff voice and tried to cover his slight embarrassment by adjusting his hat and smoothing down his cape at the front.

"Nothing boss," she said.

"Yeah.. well, just you…" he went on then shook his head as if he couldn't think how to end the comment. "Let's go."

He set off at his usual pace and Jenny let out a sigh before following in his wake. There was no way she could keep up with him, so she just made sure his black cape remained in sight and kept her legs moving. There was some relief to getting back on familiar ground and when the surrounding buildings became tenements again, she gave up following Andy and went at her own pace.

It gave her a chance to think about what she was getting herself in to. She'd already agreed to go through with the plan of being a maid at the large mansion but still wasn't sure it was such a good idea. It was too late to change her mind though, and she wondered what it would be like doing an honest day's work that paid a wage.

"Definitely a new experience for me," she let out under her breath and shook her head.

She made a vow to just get on with casing the property she would be working in as quickly as she could to let Andy know what was available. If she then saw any opportunities in the surrounding buildings, she could take advantage of them first then finish the job and get back to the life she knew. The less time she spent in the home of an aristocrat, the better as far as she was concerned. Her slow pace meant she got home almost twenty minutes after Andy, and it was him that slid open the small hatch at eye level in the door when she knocked.

"Password," he demanded.

"You can see it's me," Jenny let out in an exasperated tone.

"Password," he repeated.

Jenny let out a sigh.

"Queen Victoria lives here," she replied.

She shook her head as the hatch slammed shut and she listened to the sound of chains and bolts being loosened on the other side of the door. It eventually swung open to allow her to step inside, but closed again straight away.

"Where the hell have you been?" Andy asked.

"Some of us have short legs, you know," she answered. "We can't all stride along the street as fast as you."

She walked down the hallway as Andy locked the chains and bolts again, but he was quick to catch her up when he finished.

"You need to be at The Teahouse to see Maggie at nine o'clock tomorrow morning," he told her.

Jenny let out a groan.

"Don't make me go there," she complained. "Can't she come here?"

"No, she bloody can't," Andy replied. "The Teahouse is open to customers at nine and she has to be there. You just need to go and see her, so you can get ready for your visit to the Colwell Agency. I'm not asking you to work in the place."

The cold shiver trickled slowly down Jenny's spine at the thought of that. The idea of being a working girl servicing men at a brothel was the worst thing in the world to her, and she couldn't imagine how anyone would want to live their life like that. Letting a man get close to her was something she studiously avoided, and apart from a few fumbled experiences with boys out of curiosity, she was still naïve when it came to getting physical with the opposite sex. That didn't particularly bother her, and if she was honest with herself, the thought of losing her virginity scared her more than it excited her. She looked at Andy and saw him staring intently at her.

"OK, OK, I'll go," she told him in a disgruntled tone.

"Good girl," he said and walked off.

Jenny grimaced as she watched him disappear from view then moved in the direction of the kitchen to get some tea.

"You're back; I missed you!"

The sound of the little girl's voice stopped her and she let out a quiet laugh.

"I was only gone for a couple of hours, Lorna," she said.

The nine-year-old girl was one of Andy's newest recruits and reminded Jenny of herself when she was first brought in off the streets. Lorna took a shine to her and stuck close by whenever she was there. It could be wearying, but at the same time she understood the little girl's nervousness and remembered having the same feelings.

"Are you going to bed?" Lorna asked.

Jenny shook her head.

"Not yet," she said. "You run along and I'll be there in a while."

Lorna nodded and walked off towards the small bedroom they shared. Jenny continued walking to the kitchen and saw it was empty when she got there. The fire was burning in the hearth, and she was quick to put some water in a blackened kettle and set it in place. She watched the flames dancing around the metal as she waited for the water to boil and when it did, made herself the tea.

No one came in to disturb her, and she guessed that most of the others were already in bed or out on a job. It gave her a chance to think and she suddenly wondered if she would need to sleep at the mansion. She picked up her cup to go in search of Andy and tried the room where she thought he was most likely to be. Walking up to the small study, she knocked on the door.

"Who is it?" Andy's voice came from within.

"Jenny," she shouted.

"Come on in," he replied.

The brief exchange gave her permission to enter, so she opened the door and walked inside. Andy was sitting on a rickety wooden chair behind a small desk.

"Was it a good day?" she asked when she saw the money in front of him.

"Not good, not bad," he replied. "We have enough to keep us going and hopefully some of the girls will come back tonight with a good haul."

She heard the slight dejection in his voice and knew that the travails of looking after his gang and the others that relied on his generosity weighed heavily on him. It wasn't something he liked to show, and in truth he hid it well, but Jenny recognized the signs and picked up the inflections in his voice that gave away his concerns.

"Things will be fine," she said.

He leaned back in his seat and let out a sigh.

"I know," he said. "It's not like we have a choice anyway. If we don't do it, who will? We need to make sure that everyone is OK."

"Yeah, that's why I'm here," Jenny said.

He narrowed his eyes as he leaned forward and put his elbows on the desk. He said nothing at first, but the quizzical expression showed on his face and the question eventually came out.

"What do you mean?" he asked.

"This job you want me to do taking on the maid's role in a mansion…" she went on.

"You're not going to tell me you want to back out are you?" Andy said as he leaned further forward.

"No," Jenny replied. "But will I need to stay there… I mean sleep there at night?"

"Of course you will," he said. "Being a maid is a full time job, and that's what we want anyway. If you see any opportunities in the neighboring residences, then you'll need to make your move at night."

"That's what I thought," Jenny said. "The thing is you asked me to keep an eye on Lorna and show her the ropes to get her settled in. I won't be able to do that if I'm not here."

Andy leaned back and pressed his hands together.

"Don't you worry about Lorna," he said. "I'll get one of the other girls to look after her while you're not here."

"See that you do," Jenny said and got back to her feet.

"Well, well," Andy teased her and laughed. "It's not like our favorite stony-hearted tomboy to get sentimental about a new recruit."

"Yeah," she threw back at him with a grin. "I wonder who it was that taught me we should care about the strays we take in and look after."

"I wouldn't have a clue about that," Andy replied and smiled before his expression became serious. "Just you be at The Teahouse by nine tomorrow. Let me worry about Lorna."

"Yes, boss," were Jenny's last words to him before walking out the room.

She carried her tea back to the kitchen and finished drinking it. She then left the cup in a dirty bowl of water before making her way to the bedroom and getting undressed. Lorna was already sleeping and stirred only a bit when Jenny got in beside her to cuddle close. She considered waking the little girl up and telling her that she would be gone for…

It came to Jenny that she didn't really know how long she would be gone for, and she lay with her eyes wide open looking around in the darkness. The job in the mansion was going to be different than anything she'd done before, and she wasn't really looking forward to it. Not least of that was because it meant coming into close contact with the upper class people again. The emotional and physical scars of her last experience of that were still with her, and she didn't want any more.

"This time I come out on top," she muttered under her breath as she closed her eyes and tried to get some rest.

Chapter 3

Thomas was already awake and sitting up in when the sound of knocking on his bedroom door came to him.

"Enter," he shouted.

He watched as his butler, Stevens, came in the room carrying a tray on which there was a cup of Earl Grey tea and a newspaper.

"Did you sleep well, sir?" the elderly man asked as he moved across the room.

"I did," Thomas answered.

When the tray was set on the bedside table, he picked up the cup to take a sip of the tea then put it down again and grabbed the paper. He unfolded it to look at the headlines, but there was nothing of note that interested him and he quickly turned his attention to the inside pages. He continued drinking the tea and browsing the news as his early morning bath was run.

"Will you be attending to any patients today, sir?" Stevens asked when the job of filling the tub was finished.

"No," Thomas replied when he lowered the newspaper to look across the room. "But I will be going out later in the morning to deal with some business."

"Which suit are you planning to wear, sir?" Stevens asked.

"Hmm… just the grey one will be fine," Thomas answered.

He returned his attention to flicking through the paper and drinking his tea as the butler went to the large wardrobe. Stevens opened the ornate wooden doors and searched through the hangers to bring out a pristine charcoal grey suit. He placed it over the back of a nearby chair then set about preparing the rest of the attire his employer would need. Within minutes there was a smart white shirt, vest, underpants, socks and braces sitting on the chair, as well as a pair of polished black shoes sitting on the floor beside it.

"I'll make sure breakfast is on the table downstairs in forty-five minutes, sir," Stevens said when he was finished.

"That's fine," Thomas told him.

"When are you planning to go out, sir?" the butler went on.

"I have a one o'clock appointment," Thomas replied. "So have the carriage ready for just after midday."

"I'll inform the driver," Stevens said. "Is there anything else you need?"

"Not right now," Thomas answered.

The butler nodded his head and made his exit from the bedroom. Thomas folded up the newspaper and set it down on the tray again. He threw back the covers then dropped his feet to the floor. When he stood, he made his way across to the small enclosed area in the corner of the bedroom that housed a plumbed-in bathtub. It was one of the luxuries of having money that he enjoyed, and it made it easy to start the day with a refreshing bath. Removing his pajamas, he tested the water before stepping over the side of the tub and sitting down.

At first he just closed his eyes to enjoy the warmth of the water, but after ten minutes or so he picked up the soap to wash himself. When he was finished, he pulled the plug to let the water drain away before standing and reaching for the fresh towel draped over a rack. Once he was dry, he walked out from the enclosed space and made his way over to the chair where his clothing was laid out. He dressed quickly then moved across to the full length mirror to check his appearance.

The bespoke suit was tailored to fit perfectly but still looked a touch ungainly on his large, muscular frame. It always irked him that no matter how smart a suit was, his appearance still came across as slightly coarse, and that thought filled his mind as he stared at his clothing. He then turned his attention to his red hair and tried to smooth it down to a side shade.

"Need to get it cut," he told himself when he finished what he was doing and saw it still looked untidy.

He eventually moved away from the mirror and went back to the chair. Sitting down, he slipped on his shoes and laced them up. He was on his feet again straight after and walked over to the door to leave the bedroom. The heels of his shoes clicked on the hardwood surface of the floor as he walked towards the large stairway that led down to the ground floor.

He stopped to straighten a picture on the wood paneled wall and stood gazing at it for a few seconds. The green hills of the countryside landscape were something he hadn't seen for real in a while, and he made a mental note that he should get out of the city at some point. The fresh air would do him good and allow him to rest his mind from the reading and researching he was undertaking. The latest academic paper he was working on was almost complete, and he decided that when it was submitted to his peers, he would take a week or two off just to relax.

It was what he usually thought when he finished a paper, but it was only occasionally that he actually went through with it. He cast his mind back and realized that it was almost nine months since his last trip to the country.

"You need to do it," he told himself as he took a final look at the picture then continued on his way to the staircase.

There were actually two, with the marble steps sweeping down in a curved shape to the large lobby area. This was also floored in marble with the family crest of the Winterbourne's being the decorative centerpiece of this area of the property. It was one of the few changes that Thomas made when he bought the place to give it a more personal touch.

He turned right when he got to the bottom of the stairs and walked in the direction of the dining room. The large table was big enough to seat twelve, although Thomas mostly sat at it alone. This was a source of consternation to his parents, who were concerned that he remained a bachelor at the age of 28. They admonished him about it whenever he visited them and tried to introduce him to the refined young ladies they considered he should be meeting with a view to marrying.

The source of shame he carried around at being unable to control his baser instincts when he was treating a patient made him avoid the meetings as much as he could. He didn't want to inflict his perversions on another, but could hardly go into detail about this and explain it to his parents.

When he reached the dining room, he walked inside to the sight of the table set out for one as usual and moved to sit down. Stevens was already there and he stepped forward to take the cover off the plate. The delicious odor of bacon and eggs immediately surrounded Thomas to whet his appetite, and he picked up his knife and fork straight away to start eating.

Stevens poured him a cup of tea from the pot then walked out of the room. It left Thomas to enjoy his breakfast in silence and he easily wolfed down the food then drank the tea. He was reaching for the pot when his butler reappeared.

"Let me do that, sir," Stevens said.

Thomas relaxed back in his seat as a second cup of Earl Grey was poured and he just looked around the large, beautifully decorated room. His gaze settled on the huge cut glass chandelier above him for a few seconds, but he glanced back down when the chink of porcelain revealed that Stevens had put the pot back down on the table.

"I'll be working in the study this morning until I go out," Thomas said.

"Very well, sir," the elderly man replied. "How is your latest paper coming along?"

"It's almost done," Thomas replied. "I think another week or so of committed work should have it ready for submission to the academy."

"I'll send Jill along to clean your study now and make sure it is ready for you," Stevens went on.

"It hasn't been done?" Thomas asked.

"I'm sorry about that, sir," Stevens went on. "Since Lucy left the household it has been difficult for Jill to keep up with the workload. The size of your home really necessitates two maids to keep on top of the cleaning from day to day and ensure that everything is completed."

"The new maid," Thomas mused.

Mention of it sent his mind back a couple of days to his visit to The Teahouse brothel. He'd gone to the Colwell Agency straight after to discuss his need for a new maid with the manager, Mr. Hollinger. He'd given no further thought to it since, as he concentrated his efforts on finishing the work needed to get his paper ready.

"Is there any likelihood of an appointment being made, sir?" Stevens asked.

Thomas looked at him.

"I enquired about it a couple of days ago with the agency I use," he told the butler. "But I've heard nothing since then." He sat thinking for a few seconds before going on. "Did you tell the driver of my plans to leave the house around midday?"

"Yes, sir," Stevens informed him.

"Speak to him again and ask that he be ready for eleven thirty instead," Thomas went on. "I'll go to the

Colwell Agency first and find out what is happening with a view to getting a new maid in place."

"Very well, sir," the butler said. "Is there anything else you need?"

"Just ask Jill to be as quick as she can in cleaning my study," Thomas said.

Stevens nodded his head then retreated from the dining room to carry out the duties asked of him. Thomas picked up the cup of tea to take a sip. There would be no point in going to his study until the work of cleaning it was finished. His mind was on the reading and writing he planned to carry out in the next couple of hours before leaving the house, but the need to arrange for a new maid for his home began to interrupt his thoughts.

"You need to get it done," he let out quietly and set his mind to making sure it was sorted that day.

He slowly finished drinking the tea in his cup before getting to his feet to leave the dining room and head in the direction of his study.

Chapter 4

Lorna was still sleeping when Jenny woke up, and she got out of the bed quietly to make sure she didn't disturb the little girl. She let out a sigh as she pulled on the tomboy outfit of ragged trousers, shirt and cap that she normally wore. It gave her some relief from the early morning chill, but it was only when she reached the kitchen that she stopped shivering. The fire was already on the go in the hearth, and she immediately walked across to stand in front of it.

"Why are you still here?"

"It's not even eight o'clock yet," Jenny complained when she turned to see Andy sitting at the table with his hands around a cup. "You told me I didn't need to go and see Maggie until nine."

He said nothing in reply and she set about boiling some water. Andy just watched as she moved across to a counter and lifted a large bowl covering a plate. The loaf underneath was already starting to go moldy and she turned up her nose.

"Don't we have any fresh bread?" she asked.

"I haven't been out yet," Andy replied. "Just cut the moldy bits off and it will be fine."

She didn't want to leave the house hungry, so she just went ahead and did that. After spreading some jam on the bread, she went to make her tea then joined Andy at the table.

"How did the girls get on last night?' she asked.

Andy made a face as he shook his head.

"Came back with a little," was all he said in response.

There was silence for a few minutes as Jenny ate her bread, and it was only after taking a sip of the tea that she spoke.

"Do you think this place I'll be working in will have some good stuff?" she asked.

Andy shrugged his shoulders and lifted the cup to his mouth before answering.

"You saw the place," he said. "The man that owns it is obviously wealthy, but there's no way of knowing what he keeps in there. You'll just need to scout out the place and see what there is. I would hope some money and maybe some fine jewelry. The properties around it might be the same."

"Do you want me to steal what I can as quickly as I can?" Jenny went on.

"There's no rush," he said. "Being a maid should give you the chance to get inside all the rooms in that mansion, so just report back to me what you find. Target the properties around it first. If you see an easy opening to get in any of those, then go ahead and do it to steal what you can."

Jenny nodded her head. It was much the same as they discussed before, and she would just need to keep her wits about her and take advantage of any opportunities that came her way.

"Why are you still here?" Andy said when he saw her cup was empty.

"Alright… alright," she let out as she got to her feet and went to put her cup in a bowl of water.

"I'll meet you in The Teahouse at the end of the week," he told her. "Let's say Friday evening after six."

"I'll try and make it," Jenny replied. "And don't forget about Lorna."

She saw Andy nod his head before she walked out of the kitchen and made her way to the front door. When she was out on the street, she looked up at the building and wondered when she would be returning to it. There was no way of really knowing; all she could do was go through with the plan and hope it didn't take too long. The first task was to get to The Teahouse, so she set off through the already busy streets in the direction of the brothel.

It was ten minutes before nine when it came in sight and she stopped across from it just to watch for a few minutes. The idea of what went on inside made her shudder, but the place appeared quiet while she stood and stared at it. She finally forced her legs to move and crossed over to the building. Opening the door, she stepped inside to the sight of Maggie. The garish red hair of the older woman was piled high on her head and pinned in place as usual and her clothes were even more colorful.

"Good morning, sir," Maggie said with a grin. "I take it you are interested in learning the delights of a young lady's body and have heard that this place has the finest girls available."

"Shut up," Jenny complained as she closed the door. "You know it's me."

"Why, bless me," Maggie let out in an exaggerated show of surprise. "If it isn't young Jenny Marks, and here was me thinking it was a young gentleman coming in to be taught the ways of the world."

"Stop it," Jenny whined as she stepped across the room.

Maggie let out a piercing shriek of laughter before going on.

"You can hardly blame me for thinking you are a boy," she said. "You certainly dress like one."

Jenny pouted as she looked down at her worn clothes.

"I like the way I dress," she replied with a shrug.

"Well, it won't do for this job," Maggie went on before she turned to yell in the direction of the room behind her. "Mrs. Harper, come out here for a while. I have some business to attend to."

They were already moving towards a door when the elderly lady stepped out to come and sit at the table Maggie just vacated.

"Will you be long?" Mrs. Harper asked.

"I need to turn this..." Maggie said and motioned towards Jenny, "...into a pretty young lady."

Mrs. Harper's gaze settled on the nineteen-year-old girl and she shook her head.

"I won't hold my breath waiting on you coming back then," she said. "Is she a new recruit for this place?"

"No, I am not," Jenny let out indignantly. "I'm..."

Her words were stopped by another piercingly loud peal of laughter.

"This little one wouldn't know what to do with a man," Maggie said. "She's an innocent."

"Hey!" Jenny protested. "I am not an innoc..."

"Oh, be quiet and just keep moving," Maggie said.

Jenny squealed as her butt was spanked and it got her moving towards the door. She let Maggie pass her by when they stepped through it then followed the older woman as they moved along the hallway to a set of steps. They climbed to the first floor and walked along to a door.

When Maggie opened it, they stepped inside and Jenny saw the steam rising from the large tin bath straight away. It was obvious how things were about to get underway, but she did nothing at first but look around. It wasn't as if she was shy about getting naked in front of another woman, but she knew she was about to be transformed and wasn't all that sure she wanted to be.

"Well?" Maggie said.

"Well what?" Jenny replied.

The older woman rolled her eyes.

"Well... the bath isn't for me," she let out sarcastically. "If you're going to become the pretty young lady we need for this job, we have to get you clean and not smelling like a pig."

"I do not smell like..." Jenny started to protest, but she saw the expression on Maggie's face.

There was no choice but to get on with things, so she walked over to a chair and began to strip off her clothes. She draped them over the back of the seat and quickly moved over to get in the bath when she was naked. Maggie moved to the chair and picked up the worn trousers and shirt.

"How long have you been wearing these rags?" she asked.

"I don't remember," Jenny replied.

"Well, now is the chance for you to try something new," Maggie went on.

Jenny could do nothing but watch as the older woman walked across to the fire in the room and threw the clothes on it.

"Was that really necessary?" she asked.

"Don't tell me you're going to miss them," Maggie said and laughed. "I can't even understand why you would want to wear them in the first place. It's so undignified."

Jenny stared at the gaudy clothes that adorned Maggie's curvy figure, but she bit her tongue to hold in the sarcastic remark that almost came out. She knew that she was more than likely to get a smacked head if she said anything cheeky, so she just remained quiet. She tried to recall the last occasion she had a proper bath, but couldn't do it as she settled down in the water to enjoy the warmth. Her eyes were only closed for a second or two before the splash made her open them again.

"Find that soap and wash yourself," Maggie instructed her.

"What are you going to do?" Jenny asked as she sat up and searched around in the water to try and find the bar of soap.

"I'm going to wash your underwear."

Jenny let out a curse when the soap squirmed from her grasp so that she needed to search for it all over again. When she finally managed to find and hold on to it, she did as she was told and cleaned herself. She was washing her face when the sound of Maggie returning came to her. The soap on her face meant she couldn't open her eyes, so she didn't see the cascade of lukewarm water coming. It drenched her head to make her splutter and gasp for breath.

"Couldn't you give me a bloody warning?" she eventually managed to get out.

Maggie just laughed as she put the half empty bucket down. She then walked over to hang the damp underwear in front of the fire before returning to kneel down beside the tub.

"Sit still," the older woman said.

Jenny watched as Maggie poured out some shampoo from a glass bottle then worked her fingers through her jet black tresses. They were quickly covered in sweet smelling lather, and she sat with her eyes tightly closed as her hair was thoroughly washed.

"Are you ready... just to give you a warning?" Maggie said.

Jenny nodded and held her breath as the rest of the water from the bucket was dumped over her head to wash the soapy lather away. The scent of the shampoo clung to her afterwards.

"Well, at least you smell like a girl now," Maggie teased her. "Let's see if we can't make you actually look like one for a change."

Jenny stood up and grabbed the towel that was held out to her. She quickly used it to dry her head and body before securing it in place around her chest to cover herself. Getting out of the tub, she looked at Maggie.

"What exactly am I meant to wear then?" she asked.

"We'll get to that," Maggie replied. "Sit down at that dressing table first."

Jenny let out an exaggerated sigh as she turned to look. She could see the makeup laid out on the wooden surface.

"Do I really need that?" she questioned.

Do you want your butt spanked?" Maggie countered.

"No," Jenny let out in a dejected voice and walked over to sit down.

Maggie moved behind her then leaned forward to pick up the brush from the dressing table. Jenny grimaced as the knots were brushed from her hair and tightened her lips to hold in the cries as the stabs of pain flared.

"See... you have lovely hair," Maggie said as she continued brushing once the knots were out of it. "Well, you would if you looked after it."

Jenny stared at herself in the mirror. Her shoulder length black hair was normally tied up or hidden under a cap, but there was no doubt that having it washed and brushed gave it a luster that did look nice.

"I knew there was a pretty girl under all that dirt," Maggie joked.

Jenny said nothing as she was made to close her eyes. The application of the makeup felt strange to her, and when she eventually looked in the mirror again, she barely recognized the face she was looking at. The faint red blusher highlighted her cheeks and the light pink of the lipstick brought attention to her mouth.

"I look like I should be working here," she said.

Maggie laughed and shook her head.

"Most of the girls working here paint their faces like me," she replied.

Jenny didn't even need to look at the older woman to know that her face was heavily made up. The hint of color on her own face was nothing compared to it, and she was thankful for that. Her dark fringe was swept to the side and pinned in place.

"That's cute," Maggie said. "I knew you would scrub up well."

Jenny wasn't sure she wanted people thinking of her as cute, but it was too late to back out of what she agreed to. She stared at her face in the mirror and didn't like or dislike what she saw. It was just strange to have such a feminine appearance for a change, and it was only when Maggie spoke again that she looked away from her reflection.

"Check your underwear and see if it's dry."

Jenny got up to walk across to the fireplace. Her panties and bra were as white as she could ever remember seeing them, and while they were warm to the touch, she could also feel the slight dampness on them. That didn't really bother her, so she just put them on anyway.

"Alice is the same size as you," Maggie said. "So these clothes should fit."

Jenny turned and her eyes opened wide as she stared at the plain blue dress.

"I'm not wearing that," she squealed. "It's way too tight."

"So… it will show off your pretty curves perfectly," Maggie said. "We want you looking nice."

Jenny groaned as the dress was thrown to her.

"But…" she started although it was as far as she got.

"I can always give you something of mine to wear," Maggie interrupted.

Jenny started at the bright colors of the older woman's outfit. She remembered Andy's rule of blending in and wasn't sure she would be able to do that anywhere at all in one of Maggie's outfits. At least the navy blue dress she was holding was less gaudy and more conservative.

"Maybe I'll stick with this," she muttered and put the dress on.

She needed to wiggle her hips to smooth the blue material down into place, and it definitely clung to her curves. Moving back to the dressing table, she ducked down to look at herself and was even more amazed at what she found staring back. The contrast from her normal appearance was almost unbelievable, and it was like she was looking at a stranger. She was almost mesmerized for a few seconds before she eventually shook her head and straightened up.

"So what's the plan now?" she asked.

"Sit down and I'll tell you," Maggie told her.

Jenny walked over to the chair and tried to get comfortable in the outfit she was wearing when she sat. It was going to take some getting used to.

"OK," Maggie said. "You're going to be working for a man called Thomas Winterbourne. Andy told me he took you to see the place you'll be staying in already."

Jenny simply nodded her head.

"Well, Mr. Winterbourne is a doctor that specializes in female hysteria," Maggie went on. "I tend to call it night terrors, and there are plenty of women afflicted by it."

"I've never heard of it," Jenny said.

"You're a young girl," Maggie pointed out. "It can affect them, but it tends to be more mature ladies that suffer. It can take the form of shakes, cold sweats, uncontrolled movements of limbs and other things."

"OK, so this man treats it?" Jenny said.

"Yes," Maggie went on. "I've chatted occasionally with him when he is here, and it's not like he has a thriving medical practice as far as I can make out, but he will help ladies that come to him through family and friends."

"I can't believe he comes here," Jenny commented. "Wouldn't it be his downfall if that was found out?"

"I guess," Maggie replied. "But men have to get their relief however they can, and he can't get it from his patients. He comes here to re-enact his examination on one of the girls and she finishes him off with her hand."

Maggie wasn't about to admit that she'd been on the receiving end of one of Thomas Winterbourne's medical massages or that it was her hand that usually finished him off when he came to the brothel.

"How exactly is he treating his patients if it is making him need to use the services in a brothel?" Jenny asked.

"That doesn't matter," Maggie answered to brush the question aside. "But on his recent visit here, he let slip that one of his maids left his household and that he needed a new one."

Jenny found herself curious by what it was that Thomas Winterbourne was doing to make him come to The Teahouse for relief afterwards, but she shrugged the thought aside as she spoke.

"And that's where I come in to things."

"Exactly," Maggie went on. "The manager of the agency that Mr. Winterbourne uses is a man that enjoys the delights of The Teahouse, so he was in no position to refuse when I requested his help."

"What did you tell him?" Jenny asked.

"The story is that my niece has arrived in town and is looking for a job as a maid," Maggie said. "I informed Mr. Hollinger that I want that position to be in Thomas Winterbourne's home."

"So this Mr. Hollinger thinks I'm your niece?" Jenny said.

"That's the story, so just stick to it," Maggie replied. "I told him you would go in to the agency at eleven thirty today. Just tell him you are Jenny Green and are there to get the details of the job. I'm sure that your quick, intelligent mind can deal with anything after that."

"Do you think Mr. Hollinger suspects anything?"

Maggie shrugged her shoulders.

"It doesn't matter if he does," she said with a grin. "The last thing he wants is his wife finding out about his visits to The Teahouse, and that's what he thinks will happen if he doesn't help me. He won't give you any problems."

"Did you give him any more details about me?" Jenny asked.

"No," Maggie replied. "Simply that you were my niece looking to work as a maid in a good home and that Thomas Winterbourne's would be the perfect place."

"OK, that seems straightforward enough" Jenny said. "What time is it now?"

"I think you've been here about an hour now, so it's probably just after ten," Maggie told her.

"Where is the Colwell Agency and how long will I need to get there from here?" Jenny went on.

"Come downstairs and I'll give you the details," Maggie said.

Jenny put on the shoes and jacket she was given and followed back down to the ground floor. Mrs. Harper disappeared back to her room the minute they appeared and Maggie went to sit at the table. She brought out a piece of paper and pencil from her pocket and drew a quick map of where the Colwell Agency was located.

She handed it across when she finished and Jenny stared at it for a few seconds. The location wasn't all that familiar, but she recognized the names of some of the streets and didn't think there would be a problem in finding it. She guessed that around twenty to thirty minutes would be long enough to walk there, and Maggie confirmed that her estimate was right. That meant there was no need to rush off, so she sat down and chatted with the older woman about nothing in particular for a while longer. The business of the brothel went on around them and a few men came in.

"You better get going," Maggie eventually said. "When are you meeting Andy again?"

"He wants me to try and get here on Friday evening," Jenny replied.

"Well, I'll see you then," Maggie said to finish the conversation.

Jenny nodded then got to her feet to leave the brothel. She was uncomfortable as she tried to walk normally in the dress, but did notice while she was sitting chatting with Maggie that her appearance got her some attention from the men that came in the place. It was an unusual experience to have someone look at her in that way, and it just brought it home how naïve she really was when it came to the opposite sex.

There was no point in worrying about it though. The outfit she was wearing would be discarded as soon as the job ended, and she set her mind to the upcoming meeting she needed to be ready for. She made a couple of wrong turns before finally making it to the street where the agency building was located. The clock on a nearby church showed that it was still ten minutes before eleven thirty, but she was in no mood to wait, so she walked straight through the door when she got to it.

"Can I help you?" the receptionist asked.

Jenny put a smile on her face as she looked at the woman.

"I'm here to see Mr. Hollinger," she replied.

"Your name?" the woman went on.

"It's Jenny Green," she replied. "I'm here to see him about a maid's position."

She stood silently as her appearance was scrutinized before the receptionist got up and walked to a door.

"You can go in straight away," the woman said when she returned.

Jenny nodded her head and stepped across to the door. She hesitated for a second to take a deep breath then put a smile on her face when she walked inside the room.

"You're early," were Mr. Hollinger's first words.

"I didn't think you would mind?" she replied.

He pointed to the chair on the opposite side of the desk from him and Jenny moved across to it and sat down.

"So you're Maggie Green's niece," he said.

"Yes," she replied. "I came to stay with her and she said you would be able to help me find a job."

He narrowed his eyes as he stared across the desk at her, and she was sure he was about to quiz her more. It didn't happen, however, and he opened a drawer in the desk and took out a folder.

"You need to look at this," he said as he opened the folder and slid a piece of paper across the desk.

It appeared that Maggie was right and the threat of his secret being revealed was going to make Mr.

Hollinger just comply. She glanced down at the paper and saw the name Thomas Winterbourne on top.

"This is an important client of mine," he said. "So make sure you do a good job for him."

Jenny just nodded her head and brought her gaze up.

"When do I go to see him?" she asked.

"I'll get in touch with him and let him know that you'll arrive at four this afternoon," Mr. Hollinger went on.

"For an interview or to start work?" she went on.

"I'm sure he will have a few questions for you," Mr. Hollinger replied. "But as far as I'm concerned, we are supplying you to him to start work right away."

"How much is the pay?" Jenny asked.
"The going rate is three pounds a month," he told her. "It will be paid to you through Mr. Winterbourne. The details should be given to you once you arrive. Just fill in that form and be at the house at four in the afternoon."

Jenny almost let out a startled rush of breath but stopped herself from doing it. Her reading and writing were basic and filling out a form was something she'd never done in her life. She picked up the pencil rolled across the desk to her and got started. It turned out to be easier than she anticipated, and she just tried to finish as quickly as she could. For her name she filled in Jenny Green then she just made up whatever she could think of for the rest of the information. She suspected it would go in the file and none of it would ever be checked.

"Finished," she said when she put the pencil down.

Mr. Hollinger reached for the form and her nerves spiked when she saw him begin reading it. He made no comment when he finished and simply put the form in the file before closing it. Jenny smiled at him when he looked up.

"Make sure you are there on time this afternoon," he told her.

"I will be," she agreed. "Is there anything else you need from me?"

Mr. Hollinger shook his head then realized he hadn't given her the address. He opened the file again and brought out a piece of paper with the details on it.

"You'll need that," he said. "So you know where to go."

"Oh yeah," Jenny replied and laughed nervously. "I won't be able to get there without the address of the property, will I?"

Nothing more passed between them as she got up and walked to the door, but her hand froze on the handle when Mr. Hollinger's voice sounded out.

"And how is Maggie doing?"

Jenny knew exactly how to answer.

"She's working hard as usual, you know?" she said as she looked back.

Mr. Hollinger stared for only a second before dropping his gaze. Her comment obviously brought thoughts of The Teahouse to his mind and he said no more as she opened the door and left. Her head was bowed as she hurried across to the front door leading out to the street. All she wanted now was to get out of the place, and it made her careless. It was only at the last second that she lifted her gaze to see the man standing just outside the door about to come inside. She almost collided with him but just managed to stop herself before it happened.

"I'm so sorry," she apologized as she glanced up.

The man smiled at her and she saw the look in his eyes. It was the same as the men in the brothel when she was chatting with Maggie earlier.

"No harm done," the man said. "Just let me get out of your way."

"Thank you," Jenny replied.

It was a politeness she wasn't used to and for some reason she found it endearing.

"Have a nice day," the man said to her.

"You too," she replied and smiled.

As soon as he stepped out of her way she was on the move again, but the urge to look over her shoulder was one she couldn't resist. She immediately saw that the man was watching and quickly brought her gaze in front of herself again. When she glanced back again, she saw him stepping through the door of the Colwell Agency and the moment was gone. She put it out of her mind as she set off in the direction of Thomas Winterbourne's home. It was too early to walk all the way there, but she wandered in the general direction of the property until the sight of bread in a bakery window brought out her hunger.

It was a way to waste some time and give her a chance to prepare herself for what was to come that afternoon, so she walked inside and used the last of her money to buy herself something to eat.

Chapter 5

It was mid-afternoon when Mrs. Harper sat down at the front table of The Teahouse brothel to take over dealing with the men that came in. That gave Maggie a few hours to have a rest before she resumed her role as the Madame when the busy evening period started. She wasn't about to just put her feet up though; she wrapped a shawl around her shoulders before stepping out of the building to set off in the direction of the property used by Andy Kent and his gang of thieves.

Her mind was on the plan set in motion that day as she walked and she wondered how Jenny was getting on. She told herself that finding out was the purpose of her visit, although she knew that it was partly an excuse and there were other reasons that she wanted to see Andy. The image of his face came in her mind and made her smile, but when she realized she was doing it, she quickly wiped it away.

They were friends and occasional working colleagues more than anything else, although she knew that she would happily change that if he asked her for more. Not that he ever had, and she wasn't sure he ever would. She knew the unhappy background that led him into the world he now lived. It revolved around his gang and there didn't seem to be room for anything else.

When she arrived at the tenement building, she walked inside the darkened hallway and up to the correct door. She rapped her knuckles on the wood and waited. Seconds later the sliding hatch opened up and she didn't wait for the challenge from within.

"Queen Victoria lives here," she said.

Her words were acknowledged by the sound of the locks and chains being undone then the door swinging open to let her enter.

"Hello, Maggie," the teenage girl on the other side of it said and smiled.

"Such a pretty face," she replied as she cradled the girl's chin. "The boys must be chasing you already."

"They are not," the girl let out in a squeal and giggled.

"Well, they should be," Maggie went on teasing her and laughed. "Is your boss man here?"

"In his study, I think," the girl replied.

She closed the door and turned to walk away when the grip on her chin was released. Maggie followed on after her and stopped at the study door. She knew that anyone wanting to enter was supposed to knock first and wait to be called in, but she couldn't resist ignoring that.

"Any money for me?" she let out when she opened the door and stepped inside.

She laughed when she saw Andy shake his head and an exasperated expression crossed his face.

"Don't you follow the rules?" he asked.

"I said the password to get in the house," she countered.

"Yeah, well you're supposed to knock on the study door and wait for my shout before coming inside," Andy went on. "I could have been doing something I didn't want you to see."

"That sounds interesting," she teased him and laughed again. "Maybe one day I'll get lucky and catch you."

"Shut the door and sit," he told her.

"You're not my boss," Maggie let out. "I don't…"

"Just sit," Andy urged her. He watched as she did as he asked and only spoke again when she was sitting. "Did everything go as planned with Jenny this morning?"

"Well, she came to see me," Maggie informed him. "And I transformed her from a scruffy tomboy to a young lady."

"How did she look?" Andy asked.

"She's actually a very pretty girl," Maggie replied. "Well... once you get past the dirt and boy's clothes she usually wears that is."

"Did she complain?" Andy asked.

"What do you think?" Maggie responded and rolled her eyes. "She bellyached about wearing makeup and a dress. I'm sure she prefers people thinking she's a boy."

"You could be right," Andy said and laughed. "So, she went to the agency looking like she might actually be a maid."

"I think she'll fit in," Maggie told him.

"And how did her meeting go?" Andy asked.

Maggie shrugged her shoulders.

"I haven't seen her since," she answered. "I thought she might have come here after it, which was the reason for my visit."

"She hasn't been back here," he told her. "The last I saw of her was when I kicked her out to go and see you at The Teahouse this morning."

"Do you think she's OK?" Maggie asked.

"I wouldn't worry about Jenny," Andy replied. "She's the best girl I have working for me. That quick witted brain and smart mouth can deal with pretty much anything."

"Maybe she was just asked to go straight to the house by Mr. Hollinger," Maggie mused.

"I guess so," Andy went on. "There's no point in worrying about it now. I told her to come to The Teahouse on Friday evening if she could, and that's only a couple of days away. We should find out from her then what's going on."

"Yeah, she told me about your plans to meet," Maggie replied. "We'll just have to wait and see what happens, I suppose. I wish I knew though."

"There's nothing we can do now," Andy replied. "The scheme is set in motion and we'll just have to take it as it comes. I'm sure we'll hear soon enough if Jenny comes across any problems, and barring that we should see her on Friday evening."

"Sure," Maggie replied. "So what other plans have you got on the go at the minute?"

"Just the usual small stuff," Andy replied. "Some of the girls were out last night to break in to a property I showed them, but they didn't come back with much to be honest."

"Are the coffers drying up?" Maggie asked.

"Not quite," Andy replied. "But we could do with your plan coming off and bringing in some good money. It isn't easy feeding so many mouths and there seem to be more and more with each passing month."

"Well, someone has to do it," Maggie said in a softer tone. "Most of the poor orphan kids and single mothers around here wouldn't stand a chance if it wasn't for the help you gave them."

"Yeah, I know," Andy agreed. "But it's getting to be an expensive business these days."

"Well, maybe Jenny will get lucky," Maggie told him. "By all accounts Thomas Winterbourne is a wealthy man, so I'd suspect he must have some valuable belongings in that fancy house of his, and the same must go for the owners of the neighboring properties."

"It's what I'm hoping for," Andy replied. "So keep your fingers crossed that Jenny comes through with a good haul that will set us up for a while."

"I'm sure she will," Maggie said.

There was silence for a few seconds as if Andy was considering the riches that the scheme might bring, but he eventually spoke again.

"I was just about to make myself a pot of tea. Do you want to stay and have some?"

"Sure," Maggie answered. "I don't need to be back at work for a few hours yet. Do you need a hand making it?"

"No," Andy told her. "You just relax. I'll go and get it."

"You're going to spoil me," she teased him and laughed. "I thought you cruel criminal masterminds expected to be served hand and foot."

"I can be a gentleman sometimes," he shot back. "Just don't tell that to any of the girls here."

Maggie laughed and shook her head as he got to his feet then walked out of the room. It left her sitting alone and her thoughts returned to the plan that was her idea. Again she found herself wishing she knew what was going on with the tomboy she transformed into a pretty young lady that morning.

That wasn't going to happen, however, and it was now up to Jenny to make a success of things.

Chapter 6

The imposing metal gates of Thomas Winterbourne's mansion loomed large in Jenny's vision as she approached them and there was no stopping the onset of nerves. Memories of the last occasion she came in close contact with wealthy people of an aristocratic background flashed through her mind and it only added to the morbid sense of dread she couldn't shake off. The house she now stared at wasn't an orphanage, however, and she wasn't a nine-year-old girl any more. It didn't stop her wondering if the beatings and mistreatment she suffered as a youngster would be repeated when she walked through the gates.

"Don't be silly," she told herself, but try as she might she couldn't clear that idea from her mind.

She glanced across at the pull-rope attached to a bell and guessed it was the way to get the attention of those inside. Moving across to it, she wrapped her fingers around the rope then hesitated as she inhaled a couple of deep breaths.

"Here goes," she let out quietly and gave the rope a couple of yanks to make the bell ring.

Nothing stirred for a moment or two and the seconds stretched out to make her wonder if anyone actually heard. She considered ringing the bell again and was reaching for it when she saw the door of the property opening. The man that came out was elderly and dressed in a smart black uniform. He made his way down the wide driveway towards the gates, but remained quiet when he got to them.

"Umm… I'm here to see Mr. Winterbourne," Jenny said to get the conversation started.

"You're Miss Green?" the man asked.

The name sounded strange to her, but Jenny Green was who she was going to be while she worked in the property, so she nodded her head as she spoke.

"Yes, I was sent here by the Colwell Agency about the maid's position."

"Come on in," the man went on and used a key to unlock the gates so that she could step through them. "My name is Stevens. I'm Mr. Winterbourne's butler."

Jenny said nothing as she watched him lock the gates again.

"Follow me," he went on before moving back up the driveway.

Jenny walked after him and cast her gaze around the grounds. The driveway was bordered by lawns on either side and she could see flowerbeds, bushes and trees set in the grassed areas. She already knew the gate and stone wall bordering the property were around 8 feet high, but it wasn't something that worried her. She'd got over higher during her years of robbing properties for Andy, and she knew that if she needed to she would be able to climb the wall. She could see enough trees close to it that would make the task simple to do.

Stevens led her to the door of the property and closed it once they were inside. She glanced down at the marble floor and guessed that the design feature she was looking at was the Winterbourne family crest. It was a nice touch, but she wasn't there to admire the décor; she glanced around the lobby with the eye of a thief. In truth there wasn't that much to see, and she knew that it was only when she got a tour of the place and started working that she would get an idea of what valuables there were worth stealing.

The wood paneled walls of the hallway she was led into were covered with paintings, but that wasn't something that interested her. She wanted smaller items such as money, jewelry, watches and ornaments made of precious metal that would be easy to get in a pocket or small bag. Stevens eventually stopped outside a door and turned to her. She guessed she was about to meet the master of the house and was surprised by the upwelling of hatred that came on strongly.

"This is Mr. Winterbourne's study," the butler said.

Jenny prepared herself to meet the man inside, but a frown creased her brow when the door was opened and she followed Stevens inside. The room was empty and she looked towards the butler with a quizzical expression on her face.

"Mr. Winterbourne had some business to attend to this afternoon," he told her. "I don't expect he will be too much longer, however, so if you could just wait here for him."

"Certainly," Jenny replied and smiled.

"Just take a seat and I'll let Mr. Winterbourne know that you are in his study as soon as he returns," Stevens went on.

"Is he expecting me to be here?" Jenny asked as she moved to a chair beside the large desk and sat down.

"The message stating you would be coming arrived after he left this morning," Stevens answered. "But Mr. Winterbourne's plans for today included a trip to the Colwell Agency to enquire about his request for a new maid, so he might very well know that you are coming. I would expect him to return soon, so please just wait until he does."

Jenny simply nodded her head and watched as the butler moved back to the door and walked out. She was utterly amazed to be left in the room completely alone only minutes after arriving, but that feeling faded to one of suspicion that she was being set up to see what she did. It made her remain sitting still for a few minutes before she began to genuinely believe that Mr. Winterbourne wasn't actually there.

It was too good a chance to miss because the study in a large residence would always be one of the first places she considered looking if she was breaking in. She finally got to her feet and walked across the room to where she entered it. Cautiously turning the handle of the door, she edged it open just enough to get a view out to the hallway. There appeared to be no one there, so she popped her head out to quickly glance both ways.

Her pulse was racing, but she saw that there was definitely no one there. Hurriedly closing the door, she walked back to the desk and moved around to the opposite side from where she'd been sitting. She glanced at the papers on the wooden surface and the title in capital letters on the top page caught her attention.

'CASE STUDIES IN THE SYMPTOMS AND TREATMENTS OF FEMALE HYSTERIA'

Female hysteria was the term Maggie used when explaining what Thomas Winterbourne specialized in. She remembered being intrigued by it and quickly flicked through more pages. The medical language of what she read was dry and boring, so she gave up almost straight away. An academic paper was worth nothing to her anyway, and she turned her gaze to the drawers in the desk. They weren't locked and it allowed her to have a quick search through them. The letter opener and inkwell she saw were definitely made of silver, as were some of the fountain pens she picked up.

There was no money that she could see and nothing else of interest in the drawers. She made a mental note of the items that might be worth stealing then moved across to a small cabinet. The candlesticks inside were brass and she was sure Andy would be able to sell them for something. There were also a few medical instruments, but she had no idea if they were valuable or not. The other furniture pieces in the room included a chest of drawers, a bookcase and a drinks cabinet containing cigars and whisky.

She picked one of the bottles of alcohol out and was sure that Andy would thank her for it, although she suspected he might keep it for himself. It was as she was looking at the label that the sound of footsteps clicking on the hardwood floor came to her. It was followed by the quiet murmur of voices and there was no doubt that someone was approaching.

"Shit," she cursed quietly as she hurriedly put the bottle back where she found it and closed the drinks cabinet.

The concern lit up in her mind as she looked around, but as far as she could see everything looked the same way as when she first walked in the room. She moved back to the chair and just managed to sit down when she heard the sound of the door opening. Her heartbeat was pumping and she consciously tried to calm herself as she stared down at her feet.

"Thank you, Stevens," a voice said followed by the sound of the door closing again.

It was obviously the arrival of the man she was about to start working for and the flare of unbidden hatred welled up again. She tried to choke it down as she stood and turned to introduce herself. Her mouth opened, but no words came out as the shock hit her. The surprise showed on the face of Thomas Winterbourne too and Jenny could see that she was looking at the man she almost bumped into when she was leaving the Colwell Agency building.

"You," she eventually managed to get out, but realized that what she said was rude and stumbled over her apology. "Oh... I mean... sorry...."

The quiet laugh of Thomas stopped her words.

"Well, Mr. Hollinger did tell me that you were in his office not long before I arrived," he said. "But I didn't quite realize that the new maid would be the pretty girl that almost knocked me over."

The rueful smile spread across Jenny's face.

"I'm sorry about that," she said.

"Well, like I said this morning, there was no harm done," he went on. "I tried to get back for four o'clock, but business detained me. Please take a seat."

The politeness was there again and she couldn't help wondering if it was just an act he put on. Admittedly her experience of high-born people was limited to the year she spent in the orphanage, but the couple that owned it were definitely not kind or polite. They possessed a cruel streak that saw them take delight in humiliating and beating the children in their care. Jenny assumed that all upper class people were the same and looked down on and mistreated those less fortunate. That didn't seem to be the case with Thomas, but she was still wary of what she was getting herself into. He moved around the desk to sit also and it was him that spoke.

"So… you are Jenny Green I believe," he went on.

"Yes, sir," she replied.

"Mr. Hollinger said you have just arrived in town to stay with your aunt."

"That's right, sir," Jenny answered. "She is letting me stay with her, but I felt it was only right that I did something to help. I want to pay my way so that I'm not a burden to her."

"That's very commendable," Thomas told her. "You have worked as a maid in a large house before?"

"I have experience as a maid," Jenny told him. "Although this is the biggest house I will have worked in."

"Well I know the Colwell Agency picks its girls well, which is why I use them to find staff for my household," Thomas said. "So I'm sure you will do a fine job."

"I'll do my best, sir," Jenny replied.

"Mr. Hollinger told me you can start immediately," he went on. "Is that right?"

"Yes, I'm available right away if you need me," she told him.

"That would be excellent," Thomas said. "Is your aunt expecting you to go home this evening?"

Jenny shook her head.

"No sir," she said. "I already told her I was coming to see you and that I would be prepared to start right away. I told her that if I didn't return tonight, I would go and see her on Friday evening, if that's OK with you."

"Of course, of course," he replied. "If you need to go and see her, just come and ask me."

"Thank you, sir," Jenny said.

It seemed that getting out of the house to go and see Andy and Maggie wouldn't be such a problem. Her expectations of working in the place were already changing. She'd thought that it was going to be a challenge that would be difficult to cope with, but that didn't appear to be the case. Not that she was particularly looking forward to it, and of course her intention was still to get things over and done with as quickly as she could, but there was something about the man sitting opposite that fascinated her.

In fact it was more than that and for the first instance in her life she could sense something stirring deep inside. She wasn't quite sure what she was experiencing, but even with her limited dealings with the opposite sex, she was sure she detected an interest in her from a man. For all she knew the way Thomas was acting was how he was with all his staff, but she was certain there was something more to it. She'd been aware of some sort of a connection between them in the brief exchange they shared outside the agency building, and it seemed somehow stronger now that she was sitting directly across from him. It wasn't something she could explain to herself, but she also couldn't deny it was there. She glanced up to catch him staring at her, but she quickly averted her gaze when he went on speaking.

"Well, now that you are here," he said. "We might as well get you settled in and ready to start. My other maid is called Jill and I'll ask her to show you the ropes, so you understand your duties. She can give you a tour of the place this afternoon, introduce you to the other staff and show you the room you will be staying in."

He picked up the bell on his table and rang it loudly. The door opened not long after and she turned to see the butler walking in.

"You rang, sir?" Stevens said.

"Could you ask Jill to come to my study?" Thomas replied.

"Certainly, sir," the elderly man replied and walked out again.

Thomas got up and walked across to the chest of drawers. He reached down to open the bottom drawer and brought out a grey uniform with a white collar and cuffs.

"Do you think this will fit you?" he asked.

Jenny got up and walked across to where he was standing. She was suddenly aware of how he towered over her petite frame. His muscular body made him seem all the bigger compared to her, and she couldn't stop the slight trembling at being so close to him.

"Turn around," he told her.

She found herself obeying his command without question and she tried to control the trembling when he held the uniform against her back. It brought the touch of his hands on her shoulders and she glanced to see his slender, well manicured fingers.

"It looks like it will be fine," he said as he pulled the uniform away. "But Jill is an excellent seamstress, so if you need any adjustments just ask her."

Jenny nodded her head as she spun around. The outfit was held out to her and she took it. They were standing only a foot or so apart and it brought home to her even more how much larger Thomas was in comparison to her. She glanced up and saw him smile at her. It brought out her nerves as they gazed at each other, but the moment was broken by knocking on the door.

"Enter," Thomas shouted.

Jenny moved away from him and looked to see a pretty blonde girl walk in the room wearing a similar uniform to the one she was holding in her hands. She guessed it was Jill and that was confirmed when Thomas spoke.

"Jill, this is Jenny Green," he said. "She'll be starting today as the new maid to help you."

"Yes, sir," Jill replied.

"Could you show her around the house this afternoon and explain her duties?" Thomas went on. "Also show her the room she will be staying in and take her for something to eat in the kitchen. She can meet the others there."

"Yes, sir," Jill repeated.

Thomas turned his attention to Jenny and she was all too aware of his gaze on her.

"If there is anything else you need," he said, "Jill and the other staff will be able to assist you. Apart from that, welcome to the household."

"Thank you, sir," Jenny replied.

She walked across to where Jill was standing and was led out of the study.

"I'll take you to your room first," Jill said after closing the door.

"Sure," Jenny agreed.

She said no more and just followed after the other maid as they walked back along to the main lobby area. Jill moved over to a set of stairs in the far corner and they walked down to the lower level of the mansion.

"This is the servants' quarters then," Jenny said.

"Yeah," Jill replied. "The kitchen is down here and the rooms we sleep in."

Jenny stopped looking around. There was unlikely to be anything of interest to her in this part of the house and she wasn't planning to steal anything from the servants anyway.

Andy always drilled into her and the others he trained as part of his gang that you didn't take from those that couldn't afford to lose it. He taught them to target the wealthy and well off, and that was always the way they worked. They stole from the rich and used the proceeds to look after themselves and the unfortunates in their neighborhood that couldn't take care of themselves. Jenny knew there were plenty of people that led much better lives because of Andy's generosity in making sure they were fed and clothed. He'd saved her from the street and she was only too happy to try and do the same for others.

"This is the room you will sleep in," Jill said when she stopped at a door.

She opened it to step inside and Jenny followed. The small room was furnished with a bed, chair and a few other furniture pieces. It wasn't much different from the room she normally slept in, although she would get the luxury of having it to herself. She normally shared at Andy's home, which didn't particularly bother her, although it would be nice to sleep on her own for a change.

"Don't you have a bag?" Jill asked.

"It's at my aunt's home," Jenny lied. "I'm meeting her on Friday evening, so I'll get it then."

"Well, put on your uniform and we can get started with the tour," Jill went on.

"Sure," Jenny replied.

Getting changed in front of another girl wasn't something that bothered her either, so she quickly took off her jacket and dress then slipped the uniform over her head and let it slide down her body into place. She glanced down at herself and almost shook her head but stopped herself before she did it. Wearing a maid's outfit wasn't something she ever anticipated doing, but it was all part of the plan, so she just accepted that she needed to get on with it.

"It looks a bit big for you," Jill commented.

"It's fine," Jenny replied. "I don't really want it any tighter on me."

"Well, if you want me to take it in for you, just say," Jill went on.

"OK," Jenny agreed.

She wasn't planning to say anything. If things worked out like she planned, she wouldn't be around long enough to worry about whether the uniform fit her properly. It was the tour she was about to get that was on her mind. It would provide her with a first chance to see around the place and hopefully give her an idea of where to concentrate her efforts in the coming days to find the valuables that would be worth taking.

"So… where do we start?" she asked.

"We might as well just go to the kitchen first," Jill said. "It's where Stevens and the cook, Matilda, will be. I can introduce you to them and we can take it from there."

Jenny nodded her head and they left the bedroom to head back in the direction of the stairs they came down. Jill pointed out a door that opened to a small washroom and explained that it was for the use of the staff. She then led the way to the kitchen. It was large, with a black cooking range standing against the wall opposite the door and pots and pans hanging on hooks around it. She saw Stevens sitting at a dining table that looked big enough to seat six and beside him was a rotund woman that was obviously the cook, Matilda.

Jill made the introductions and they walked across to sit down. Jenny easily answered the questions thrown at her to make herself out as a quiet girl from a rural background that had just arrived in the big city. The other three were friendly and straight away she knew that they wouldn't be a problem to her. She just needed to make sure they didn't find out what her true intentions for being in the house were, but she was sure they wouldn't suspect her of being anything other than a cleaning maid.

Matilda made tea and sandwiches for them and they sat chatting as they ate. Keeping her guard up to make sure she didn't reveal anything that she shouldn't meant that Jenny couldn't fully relax, but she and Jill finished eating quickly and moved on. She was shown the utility room at the rear of the kitchen where the cleaning equipment was stored before they made their way back to the upper levels of the property.

She made sure to listen to what Jill was saying as she was led in and out of rooms, but she was also keeping an eye out for anything that might be of interest to Andy. There were a few small ornaments that looked promising in the main lounge, and she suspected that there might be some fine cutlery and other pieces stored in the chest of drawers in the dining room. She was even more alert when they went upstairs because she knew from experience that most people kept jewelry and money in the bedroom.

The large box on the dressing table in the main bedroom was definitely something worth investigating when the chance arose, although she didn't notice anything as promising in the guest bedrooms. She still planned to have a closer look when she got the chance to work on her own, but there was nothing she could really do other than look with Jill by her side.

"What's up there?" Jenny asked when they got to the end of a hallway on the first floor and she saw a set of stairs.

"That's the examination room where Mr. Winterbourne administers to the patients that visit the house," Jill told her.

"Can I see it?" Jenny asked.

"Sure," Jill agreed and led the way up.

Jenny didn't really think there would be anything of value in the room, but she was still curious about the treatment Thomas Winterbourne gave the women that visited him for help. That he needed to visit The Teahouse for some relief afterwards made her sure there was an intimacy to the therapy, and she wondered just what it was he was doing that would get him in such a state of arousal that he risked his reputation by visiting an east end brothel. Her eyes opened wide when she walked in the room and saw the large examination table that dominated the space. The straps at each corner were obviously used as a way of tying someone in place, and she wondered if they were used on patients.

"Does Mr. Winterbourne treat a lot of people?" she asked as she circled around the room.

"Not really," Jill replied. "As far as I can make out, he is more interested in the theory of medicine rather than the practice of it. I usually know when someone is due to arrive, though, because that's when I get asked to clean this place. It happens maybe once or twice a week at the most."

Seeing the place where Thomas administered his medical therapies only piqued Jenny's interest in finding out more. Maggie wouldn't say when she asked about them, and she guessed if she was going to discover anything, it would be in the room she was now standing in. She really needed to investigate it alone and made a vow to do just that as soon as she could.

She suddenly realized they were probably high enough in the property to easily see over the border wall, so she moved across to the single window in the room. The scene she cast her gaze out onto overlooked the property next door, and the sight of the small open window in the building caught her attention straight away. It was high enough off the ground that the owners probably thought it was safe to leave it open, but she knew better. It might be small, but so was she, and she was sure she could get to it and through it. Checking if the window was kept open was another reason to get back to the examination room on her own, and she made up her mind to do it before she went to the meeting in The Teahouse on Friday, which was a couple of days away. She turned back to Jill.

"So what do we do now?" Jenny asked.

"I've already finished most of what needed to be done today," Jill replied. "You can just relax if you want. The working day gets underway at seven, so it's just a case of getting yourself ready to start tomorrow."

Jenny nodded and they moved to the door to make their way back downstairs.

"Is it OK to have a look around the gardens?" Jenny asked when they were back at the lobby.

"It's not something I do much," Jill said. "But you can if you want."

"How do I get back in?" Jenny asked.

"Just ring the bell," Jill told her. "It will most likely be Stevens that answers it. I'll tell him you've gone outside when I return to the kitchen."

"Thanks," Jenny replied and walked to the door to let herself out.

She wasn't remotely concerned with the appearance of the garden, but she was interested in the layout. Moving around to the side of the mansion where the examination room overlooked the neighboring property, she checked if there was an easy way to climb the wall. There was a tree in the corner of the garden close enough to provide a way over, and she walked across to lean against it. She reckoned getting up wouldn't be a problem, and that would just leave her needing to find a way to reach the small window in the neighboring property.

There was no point worrying about that now, so she continued on her circuit around the grounds. She stopped every so often as if she was enjoying the sight of a plant or flower and wandered slowly to make it look like she was just admiring the scenery. Her mind was working overtime though. The sound of barking dogs alerted her to the fact that the neighboring property on the other side of the mansion may not be such an easy target. The loud sound testified to the large size of the dogs, and her first instinct was to avoid the place, but there was no point in making rash decisions. She would make a plan in the next couple of days and pass it on to Andy on Friday night.

When she completed a full circuit of the building and arrived back at the front door, she walked down the driveway and looked through the gates. The street was quiet and she saw no one walking by. It could only be just after five o'clock, and it was a good sign that the neighborhood would be deserted in the dead of night. That should make carrying out a robbery easier to do, but she put the idea out of her mind as she turned to go back inside.

Jenny stopped in her tracks when she saw the front door already open and Thomas moving onto the driveway. She saw the cigar smoke he puffed out and wondered if he always came outside to smoke. There was no avoiding him, so she simply walked back towards the property.

"Trying to escape already?" he asked.

Jenny smiled and shook her head.

"I finished my tour with Jill and she said it would be OK to have a look around the gardens," she replied. "They are beautiful."

"I'd like to say that's down to me," Thomas said. "But I have an excellent gardener that comes in a couple of times a week. I like the place looking neat and tidy, but have no real desire to get my hands dirty."

"Your gardener does a good job," Jenny said. She watched as Thomas took another puff on the cigar. "Don't you like the smell?" she went on.

"The smell of the cigar?" he asked.

Jenny nodded her head.

"Because you came outside to smoke it," she said. "I thought you might not like the smell in your home."

"I don't mind," he answered and laughed. "But sometimes I just need to get away from the work in my study and take a break. It helps me think more clearly, and a cigar seems like a good idea when I'm doing it."

"Well, I better not disturb you then," Jenny told him. "Goodnight."

"Goodnight," he replied.

She walked past him to go back inside the house and a glance over her shoulder showed that he was watching her in the same way as when they parted after their first encounter outside the agency building. It was something new for her to get the interest of a man, and she guessed it was down to the transformation from her usual tomboy appearance to pretty teenage girl. She wasn't quite sure how she felt about the attention, but it wasn't as if she didn't like it.

Moving back down the stairs to the servants' quarters, she heard the voices as she approached the kitchen. She stopped to listen, but it was simply small talk between Stevens and Matilda about work in the house. It seemed only right that she told the butler that she got back inside the house, so she stepped up to the open door and waited for a lull in the conversation.

"Mr. Winterbourne let me back inside," she said and saw the heads turn to her.

"He must be smoking a cigar then," Stevens said.

Jenny smiled and nodded her head when she spoke.

"He said he needed a break to clear his head."

"He does it most evenings about this time," Matilda told her.

Jenny looked at the clock on the wall to see it was almost six o'clock.

"I'm just going to get some rest," she went on. "I'll be up and ready to start at seven tomorrow."

"Make sure that you are," Stevens said.

Jenny turned away from the kitchen to walk to her room and let herself in. The first thing she did after closing the door was take off the grey uniform, and it left her standing in just her underwear. She decided to get under the covers of the bed to keep warm, and as she lay with her eyes closed, she went over the events of the day. She'd come in to a well-to-do home expecting to despise being there and eager to get out of it again as quickly as possible, but unbelievably that wasn't the case.

Her mind was still focused on the real work of why she came to the mansion, but it was another thought that kept surfacing to interrupt that. Her contempt for the upper classes led her to believe that she would hate the man she was working for without question. That wasn't the case however.

It wasn't hate she felt for Thomas Winterbourne. It was something altogether more unexpected.

Chapter 7

Jenny thought her first night alone in a long while would be relaxing, but being in bed on her own just felt strange to her and in the end she didn't get much sleep. When the hands of the wall clock showed six in the morning, she decided to get up. Putting on her uniform, she left the bedroom and walked along to the washroom Jill showed her the day before. The large barrel of water in the corner of the room was cold, but she filled a jug from it and poured it in the smaller basin on a stand.

A glance in the mirror above the stand showed faint traces of the makeup Maggie put on her the day before, and she cleaned her face to remove them. She then took off her uniform and hung it up before splashing water on her body. It made her shiver and she quickly grabbed the towel hanging on the stand to dry herself. After putting her uniform back on, she looked in the mirror again to smooth her hair down. When she considered it was as neat as she was going to get it, she emptied the basin before leaving the washroom. Only Matilda was in the kitchen when she walked in and the older woman smiled at her.

"Couldn't sleep?" the cook asked.

"Not really," Jenny admitted.

"It takes a while to get used to a new place," Matilda said. "Sit down and I'll make you some something to eat."

Jenny did as she was told and just watched as the cook went about her business. In a matter of minutes, a cup of tea and a plate of toast were sitting in front of her and she hungrily tucked in to them. She was already finished when Stevens came in, and it was around ten minutes more before Jill showed her face. The chatter was pleasant and she joined in as she waited for the working day to start. That only happened when her fellow maid finished her breakfast and got to her feet.

"Ready?" Jill asked.

"Yes," Jenny replied. "Do we have any paper and pencils?"

"What for?" Jill went on.

"I just want to keep a note of the routine, so I can stick to it in future," Jenny answered.

She was always amazed at how easily lying came to her because that's what she was doing. The paper and pencil was to keep a note of something, but not the routine. She wanted to make a list of valuables that she could give to Andy to let him decide what was best to steal. In any other properties she targeted, it would just be a case of grabbing what she could get her hands on when she was inside, but there was a chance in Thomas Winterbourne's home to carefully check what was available and provide her boss with the details.

"I think I have what you want," Matilda said. She walked across to a large dresser and opened a drawer to search through. Her hand came back out clutching a small notebook and a stub of a pencil. "Will these do?" she went on.

"Perfect," Jenny replied and went to get them.

She and Jill then walked to the storeroom at the back of the kitchen to collect the cleaning equipment they needed. Following this they made their way to the stairs and up to the lobby area of the property.

"First thing every morning is to get the dining room cleaned and ready for Mr. Winterbourne to have his breakfast," Jill said.

Jenny made a show of writing dining room in the notebook before they walked along to it. She was instructed to wipe down the table, chest of drawers and other furniture pieces while Jill mopped the floor and between them they finished quickly.

"OK," Jill went on. "Now we set the table."

Jenny took a real interest when they moved across to the chest of drawers. Her colleague began opening the drawers to take out a plate, cutlery and other dining accoutrements. They were nice pieces, but not the finest, and she decided to see if she could get Jill to show her more.

"Are these just used for Mr. Winterbourne or for guests as well?" she asked.

"Just for Mr. Winterbourne," Jill answered. "On the occasions that guests dine here, the silver service is used."

Jenny's ears pricked up at the mention of silver.

"That sounds special," she went on.

"Oh it is," Jill said.

She opened the very bottom drawer to take out a beautiful wooden case. Jenny moved closer and saw the rows of silver knives, forks and spoons set out inside the box when it was opened.

"The table must look good when that is set out," she said.

"It does," Jill told her. "It doesn't happen much though. It's usually only when Mr. Winterbourne's parents visit."

"How often do they come?" Jenny asked.

"Maybe once every two months," Jill answered as she closed the case and put it back.

That was good news for Jenny. It would mean it was possible to take the silver cutlery out of the box and it probably wouldn't be noticed for a while. A glance in the bottom drawer before it was closed showed her a silver milk jug, and she guessed there would be other pieces there also. She turned away before Jill saw her looking and moved across to the table.

"Which seat does Mr. Winterbourne sit at in the morning?" she asked.

She was shown by her colleague and they set it out with the pieces they were holding.

"Now we carry on with the downstairs rooms," Jill said. "I'll do the study and you do the lounge."

Jenny nodded her head. That was perfect for her, since she already knew what there was in the study and being alone in the lounge would give her a chance to look around. As soon as she walked in the room, she used a mop to clean the floor. She then used a duster on the furniture to take a closer look at the ornaments she saw the previous day. The best of them was an engraved box standing on a small tray, with both being gold plated. She opened the box and used the duster as if she was cleaning it, but there was nothing inside. There were a few pottery vases that looked antique, but she wasn't sure they were something Andy would be interested in. Before she left the lounge, she got out the notebook and wrote down the details of what she'd seen so far. She then went to find Jill in the study.

"What next?" she asked.

"When Mr. Winterbourne comes down, we go upstairs to clean his bedroom," Jill said. "After that we can have a short break before carrying on. There's a schedule in the kitchen of the other rooms that we clean each day. Most aren't used unless there are guests, so they only get cleaned a couple of times a week to make sure they are kept tidy."

It was around nine o'clock when Mr. Winterbourne made his way down and into the dining room. Jill led the way up the stairs to the main bedroom. Jenny's gaze was on the large box on the dressing table the minute she walked in the room. There was no way she could look inside while Jill was there, but her hope was that it contained some nice jewelry. She was instructed to make the bed and got on with doing it while her colleague mopped the floor. They both then worked around the furniture with dusters to finish the job.

They then made their way back down to the kitchen and sat chatting while they enjoyed a drink and something to eat. Jill showed her the cleaning schedule afterwards and they split the rooms that were to be done that day between them. It suited Jenny to be left working alone, and she collected the equipment she needed from the storeroom and set off. The rooms she was to clean were all located on the first floor of the property, and that gave her the chance to look around some more.

A guest bedroom was where she decided to start, and that was because it was close to the stairs that led up to the examination room. She completed the work quickly and looked around then stopped to listen when she came back out to the hallway. The place was quiet and she suspected she was the only person on the first floor. It was too good an opportunity to miss, so she hurried up the stairs and let herself in the door at the top. She leaned back against it as she looked around and her gaze came to rest on the large medical table. It sent a shiver trickling down her spine as she imagined Thomas Winterbourne treating a patient.

"What is it that you do?" she mused when she walked across to the table and stroked her hand across the leather surface.

The thought of getting on the table surfaced in her mind, but she resisted it to move across the room and look outside. A smile spread across her face when she saw the small window in the neighboring property was open. She was beginning to suspect that it was left like that permanently, which was exactly what she needed. It would give her a chance to get inside, but there was no rush to do it yet.

She turned away from the view and moved across to the large wardrobe against the wall. Opening one of the wood-paneled doors got her the sight of three white coats inside. They were obviously what Thomas wore when he was dealing with a patient. A glance down showed her the boxes stored in the bottom of the wardrobe, and it stirred an idea in her mind. If she really wanted to know what happened in the privacy of the examination room, she would need to be there when a patient was.

She let a grin spread across her face as she tried to shake the images from her mind. Hiding in the wardrobe to get a glimpse of Thomas treating a patient was a bad idea, and she knew that Andy would go mad that she was even contemplating it. There was no doubt if she was caught she would be immediately dismissed from the house, but even the prospect of that happening couldn't make her stop thinking about actually doing it.

"Get moving," she urged herself.

A quick look through the boxes confirmed her first instinct that there was nothing of value in the room, and she closed the wardrobe doors and walked back to the table. The image of her tied down on it flashed through her mind and the rush of her pulse was unexpected.

"Get moving," she repeated in a firmer voice.

Walking to the door of the room, she eased it open and listened. All was still quiet, so she made her way down the stairs. She collected her equipment and moved on to the next room she was to clean. It was one of the larger guest bedrooms, and she spent over an hour working in it. That gave her the chance to look around properly, but there was really nothing worth stealing. It was almost lunchtime when she walked back out the room, so she made her way downstairs.

"How did you get on?" Jill asked.

"One room left to get done," Jenny replied.

"Well, take your time and do it properly," her work colleague went on.

"I will," Jenny assured her.

After having something to eat, she returned to her duties. She already suspected there would be nothing in the bedrooms she was cleaning and found that she was right. The best prospect was still the box sitting on the dressing table in the main bedroom, but until she got in the room on her own, there was no way of knowing what was inside it.

The chance to find out came the very next morning. Mr. Winterbourne came down for breakfast earlier and they were just finished cleaning and setting up the dining room when he did.

"You just go up and get started in Mr. Winterbourne's bedroom," Jill told her. "I'll clean the study then come up and join you."

"Sure," Jenny agreed.

She needed to pick up some equipment from the kitchen and hurried down to get it before making her way up the stairs to the first floor. As soon as she was in the bedroom, she made her way over to the dressing table with a duster in her hand. She cleaned the top of the box then glanced over her shoulder towards the door. Her ears were attuned to picking up the slightest sound, but the place was quiet and she turned her attention back to the box. Her eyes opened wide when she lifted the lid to see the contents.

"Oh my god," she let out under her breath.

She picked out a string of pearls that on its own was probably worth a fortune, and the necklace was just one of many pieces. They were definitely for a lady and she wondered who they belonged to, but in the end it didn't really matter to her. A nervous glance over her shoulder showed that she was still alone and she quickly made a note of the contents of the box in the small book she'd been given. It was by far the richest pickings in the house and everything else she'd seen paled into insignificance compared to it.

She hurriedly finished what she was doing and closed the box. Her hands were shaking as she put the notebook back in her pocket and moved across to start making the bed. It wasn't long after that Jill arrived to help and Jenny tried to act normal. There was no getting her mind off the contents of the box, though, and she wondered just how much money the jewelry was worth.

It was only when she sneaked up to the examination room in the afternoon that she forgot about what she'd seen that morning. What she thought about then brought out her nerves, but the idea of being tied down to the table was an image she couldn't get out of her head. That she was fantasizing about Thomas was something that concerned her, but she couldn't stop doing it while she was in the room. The real reason she was there was to check if the window in the adjacent building was still open, and when she saw that it was, she knew it was the first property she was going to target.

After leaving the examination room, she got on with finishing her work for the day then made her way down to the servants' quarters. What she needed to do now was get away from the property to go to The Teahouse, but she waited until just after six before she made her move.

"I have to go and meet my aunt to pick up some belongings," she told Stevens. "I asked Mr. Winterbourne already if I could go and he said it was OK, so could you let me out please?"

The elderly butler nodded his head and got up from where he was sitting at the kitchen table. Jenny followed him up the stairs and saw she was right to have waited when they walked out the already open door. Thomas was standing on the driveway smoking a cigar and he smiled as he saw them coming. She immediately thought of that afternoon's fantasy about him and could barely look at him, but forced herself to do it and returned his smile.

"Off to see your aunt?" he asked.

She was surprised he remembered her telling him and wondered if it was a sign of his interest.

"Yes," she replied. "I won't be long."

"There's no rush," he replied. "I'm sure that your aunt will be pleased to see you."

"Thank you," Jenny said.

She glanced to see him smile at her again and the slight twinge of guilt struck her unexpectedly. In all her years of stealing for Andy, she never once felt remorse at what she was doing or the merest shred of sympathy for those she stole from. Then again, she never actually knew any of them and was usually in and out their houses in a matter of minutes. That was different with Thomas; she was actually getting to know the man she was going to rob.

The twinge of guilt wasn't something she wanted to feel, and she tried to brush it away as she moved past him and down towards the gate. She needed to keep her mind on the matter at hand, and that was making sure her gang got the money they needed to survive. What she was doing would also help the others that Andy looked after.

It was that thought she tried to keep on her mind when she moved through the gate being held open by Stevens and set off along the street into the growing darkness of early evening.

Chapter 8

The door of The Teahouse brothel swung open and Maggie watched as the man came in then moved towards the table she was sitting at. She kept her face straight as she spoke.

"We have some lovely girls here, sir," she said. "They'll give you everything you want."

"I'm sure you do," Andy replied and shook his head. "But there's only one girl that can give me what I want. Is she here?"

Maggie shook her head.

"No sign of Jenny yet," she answered. "Was it six o'clock you agreed to meet?"

"I asked her to try and get here after six," Andy replied. "So I'm not sure what time she'll turn up. It depends how easy it is for her to get away."

"Well, just sit down then," Maggie told him.

They both looked towards the door at the sound of it opening, but it was to the sight of Samantha coming in. She motioned her head towards Andy as she stepped across to the table, but it just got a laugh from the Madame of the brothel.

"This one is with me," Maggie said.

"Is it busy yet?" Samantha asked.

"No," Maggie replied. "You stick by me just now because I will likely need you to take over here for a while."

"Can't Mrs. Harper do it?" Samantha complained. "I won't make any money sitting out here."

"Mrs. Harper just finished the afternoon shift," Maggie said. "All I'll need is for you to take over for a short while and I'll make sure you get something for doing it."

The offer of some money was enough to get Samantha to agree and she dropped down on a seat. It was twenty minutes before Jenny eventually came through the front door and Maggie and Andy were on their feet straight away.

"Do you have somewhere private?" Andy asked.

"Of course," Maggie replied.

She led the way along a ground floor hallway and the door she opened brought them into a small lounge. Closing it again when all three of them were inside, she motioned for them to sit on the chairs around a small table.

"So how did it go?" Andy asked.

"Well... I'm working as a cleaning maid in a mansion," Jenny replied.

"They don't suspect anything?" Maggie asked.

Jenny shook her head.

"No," she answered. "As far as I can make out, they just think I'm an agency maid."

"Did you have any problems getting out of the house to come here?" was Maggie's next question.

"Nope," Jenny told her. "I told them I needed to see my aunt and the gate was opened to let me out. It was as simple as that."

"And what's in that fine house?" Andy asked.

The smile broke out on Jenny's face.

"Oh there is plenty that I think you'll like," she said. "I wrote it down for you."

"Good girl," Andy praised her.

Jenny got the notebook out and ripped out the pages where she wrote down the things she'd seen in Thomas Winterbourne's house. She handed them across and was silent as Andy read it.

"This is a treasure trove," he let out when he looked up at her.

"Let me see," Maggie cut in and grabbed the pages from him.

"We've got to have that jewelry," Andy said with a grin.

"I know," Jenny agreed. "The other things in his home are nice, but those necklaces, rings and bracelets must be worth a fortune."

"What are the pearls like?" Maggie asked.

The note of excitement was all too apparent in the older woman's voice.

"It made me shake just holding them," Jenny said. "I've never seen anything like it."

"What about the surrounding residences?" Andy said.

"I think I've seen a way into the house next door," Jenny told him. "But I need some things if I'm going to try breaking in."

"What?" Andy asked.

"Well, Maggie burned my old clothes," she said. "All I have now is a dress and a maid's uniform. There's no way I can climb over a wall and get in a house wearing them. I need a pair of pants, a shirt and a cap in dark colors."

Andy looked to Maggie.

"Can you arrange for that?" he asked her.

"I think so," she replied and got to her feet. "Give me a few minutes or so and I'll see what we have here."

Jenny and Andy watched her leave the room and it was the teenage girl that spoke first when they were alone.

"I want to get started," she said. "My plan is to hit the building next door tonight. It's the one on the right hand side of the mansion when you are looking at it from across the street."

"How will you get in?" Andy asked.

"As far as I can see, they leave a small window always open on the side of the property," Jenny told him. "I think I can get over the wall and up to it as a way inside."

Andy nodded his head.

"What do you intend to do with the things you steal?" he asked her.

"I don't want to keep them with me," she replied. "It's too risky. You need to arrange for one of the other girls to be at the gates of that house around two o'clock in the morning. I'll be finished by then and will pass on whatever I get."

"OK, I'll make sure someone is there," he said. "What about the other neighboring properties?"

Jenny shrugged her shoulders.

"I can hear dogs in the house on the other side of the mansion, so not sure there is much chance of getting in there," she replied. "I haven't had the chance to look further afield. I was just concentrating my efforts on finding out what was available in Thomas Winterbourne's home."

"What's he like?" Andy asked.

Jenny hesitated and wasn't quite sure what to say. She would have loved to describe him as a nasty, pompous, self-important pig that she detested and had not the slightest ounce of compassion for. It was the image she built up in her mind before entering the property, but she now knew that wasn't the case. The truth was that he was a decent man and she remembered the guilt that pricked in her conscience when she was leaving the residence that evening.

She knew Andy would think she'd gone soft if she admitted Thomas Winterbourne fascinated her and was a man that brought out feelings in her that she couldn't explain to herself.

"Well…?" Andy prompted when the silence stretched out.

Jenny shrugged her shoulders and realized she was taking too long to answer.

"He's upper class," she said. "You know how I feel about them. To be honest, I don't see much of him, which is fine by me."

She was saved from any more questions by the door opening and Maggie reappearing.

"This is the best I can do," the older woman said.

Jenny got up from where she was sitting and went to look at the clothes.

"They'll do," she said. "Do you have a bag?"

"Sure," Maggie said. "Is there anything else?"

"No," Jenny said. "I just need something to hide these clothes in. It will look a bit suspicious if I'm seen returning with boy's clothing."

Maggie nodded as she disappeared from the room again.

"So you rob the first property tonight and then what?" Andy asked.

"I'll check what other opportunities there are and let you know," Jenny said.

"Well, be quick about it," he told her. "I think we just need to finish this job and steal the jewelry box. If it's as good as you make out, it should set us up for a long while."

"What about the other things on the list?" she asked him.

"If you can get them, then do it," he told her. "But the jewelry is the number one target. If that is all you can get, then fine. I'd be more than happy with that."

No more was said when the door opened and Maggie came back in. She got the clothes to put them in the small black bag she was carrying and handed it over.

"I better get going," Jenny said. "Remember to have someone at the gates of that house tonight at two."

"Don't worry," Andy assured her. "Someone will be there."

Jenny gave him a quick smile and stepped out of the room to the hallway. She walked back in the direction of the front door, but turned back before she left.

"When do you want to meet again?" she asked.

"Let's say on Monday evening around six o'clock," Andy told her.

Jenny acknowledged the comment with a curt nod then walked out of the brothel and set off at a brisk pace to walk back to the mansion.

"Do you think she'll be alright?" Maggie queried.

"She'll be fine," Andy replied. "This job is going to be our best ever."

"It looks like it going by what I read on that list," Maggie went on.

Andy said no more as he left and he caught a last glimpse of Jenny turning a corner in the darkness. She kept her eyes on the ground in front of her as step after step brought her closer to what was effectively now her home. It was strange to think of Thomas Winterbourne's mansion like that, but as she continued walking she caught herself wondering if it would be so bad if it really was her home.

"Stop it," she snapped. "Remember why you're there."

She suddenly realized how loud she spoke, but a glance around showed no one close enough to hear what she said. For the rest of the walk back to the property, she forced herself to think about the robbery she was planning to carry out that night. There were still hours to go before she planned to make a move, but the familiar rush of adrenaline was already starting to take hold. She tried to contain it, but her pulse was racing when she got back to the gates of the mansion.

"Keep calm," she let out under her breath and inhaled a couple of long, deep breaths before grabbing the pull-rope to ring the bell.

It was a few minutes before Stevens came out of the front door and walked down the driveway to the gates. He unlocked them and Jenny thanked him as she quickly stepped through.

"How is your aunt?" he asked as he closed the gates and relocked them.

Jenny waited until he finished the task and they started walking up the driveway before answering.

"My aunt is fine," she replied. "It was good to see her."

"Will you be going to visit her again?" the butler went on.

"Maybe," Jenny told him. "She did ask me to go to her home on Monday evening, but I told her I wasn't sure I could make it. I'll see how work goes in the next few days and ask Mr. Winterbourne if it's OK."

"I'm sure he won't mind," Stevens told her. "As long as your work for the day is finished before you leave."

Jenny just nodded her head as they walked inside. She waited for Stevens to close and lock the door before they made their way down to the servants' quarters.

"I'll see you in the morning," she said when they reached the kitchen door.

"Goodnight," Stevens replied.

It was the last of the conversation and she walked towards her room. When she got inside she was quick to strip off the clothes she was wearing and got under the covers on the bed. The clock on the wall showed it was just after eight thirty, so she tried to get some rest. She didn't want to close her eyes for fear that she would fall asleep, so she just lay in the darkness going over what she was going to do that night. Thoughts of her employer kept intruding and it began to annoy her.

"Try and focus, Jenny," she hissed, but she continued to think about Thomas Winterbourne as much she did the robbery she was about to commit.

It was only when she got out of bed as it got to fifteen minutes before one that she was able to concentrate completely on the job she was about to do. She wasn't sure if that was wholly down to putting on the clothes Maggie gave her, but the tomboy outfit definitely got her thinking like the thief she knew she was. Moving to the door of the bedroom, she eased it open and listened for a few minutes. The house was still and it allowed her to slip out to the hallway and quietly close the bedroom door.

Jenny stuck close to the wall as she moved in the darkness towards the stairway. She climbed to the lobby area and stopped again to listen. There was only silence around her, so she moved along the ground floor hallway to the small lounge at the end of it. The adrenaline was really flooding her veins now, and when she was inside the room, she stopped to take a few deep breaths. Moving to the window, she opened it as a way outside and made sure it was secured in place once she was standing on the grass. She needed it to stay open as a way back inside.

Quickly moving to the tree in the corner of the garden, she bent down to dirty her hands then wiped them on her face. It blackened her pale skin and helped her fade into the darkness around her. Climbing the tree wasn't difficult, and once she was high enough, she inched along a branch until she was close enough to grab hold of the top of the wall. She didn't want to stay on it and exposed for too long, but took the opportunity to look around and check for a way back over the wall when she was finished.

There were no trees available, but a long wooden box standing against the wall looked high enough to help her get back up onto the top. As far as she could see, it was the best option, so she quickly lowered herself down until she was hanging by her fingertips then let go and dropped to the ground. The grass deadened the sound of her landing, but she remained crouched down for a few seconds just to make sure that nothing stirred. When she was sure that she hadn't been heard, she straightened up and raced across to get in the shadows at the side of the building.

She got herself directly under the small open window, and it looked a lot higher to her now than when she was staring at it out of the examination room. Finding a way to get up to it was the next task; she glanced around her. She reckoned the long wooden box was likely filled with garden tools and took the chance to see if there was anything in it that might help. The sight of the short wooden stepladder was just what she wanted and she removed it from the box as quietly as she could. Moving back to the side of the building, she set the ladder up and climbed it. At a stretch she could now reach the window and she grabbed hold of the sill to pull herself up. It wasn't exactly easy to get inside, but she was practiced enough in the art to manage it.

She was on the first floor of the property and that was risky. The occupants were more than likely sleeping in the bedrooms and she crept past them as quietly as she could to get to the staircase. She let out a slow breath when she got downstairs. The house was dark to show there was definitely no one up, and she started moving to doors and opening them to look inside. When she got to what looked like a study, she moved inside it and closed the door. She struck lucky straight away when she saw a watch with a long chain attached to it sitting on the desk.

"Nice start," she let out as she picked it up and pocketed it.

Moving around the desk, she crouched down to open the drawers. The roll of banknotes hidden at the very back of the top one brought a grin to her face and she found a few fountain pens in the next. There was nothing else of any value in the other drawers, so she quickly closed them and moved on. Stepping across to a small cabinet, she opened it to see some ornate candlesticks. They were too big to put in a pocket, and she debated taking them before finally deciding not to. The sensible thing was to keep looking and if she couldn't find anything else, she could always come back for the candlesticks later.

She walked back to the door and pressed her ear against the wood to listen before opening it. She moved on to the rest of the downstairs rooms and filled her pockets with whatever she could find. They were stuffed to bursting when she finished, and she knew it was time to get out. The clock on the wall of the room she was in showed that it was now fifteen minutes before two. The girl coming to see her would more than likely be close by and she considered her options for getting out.

In the end, there was only one and she knew she needed to leave the property the same way she came in. Moving to the bottom of the stairs, she stopped to listen for any noise. The darkened house was still and she stealthily made her way up the staircase and along the hall to the window. She glanced out to see the top of the stepladder a long way below and knew that she would need to go out through the window feet first. It wasn't the easiest of ways to make an exit, and the concern was that she would make a noise that would wake up the occupants.

Jenny tried to calm her breathing as she climbed up on the window sill then slid her feet and legs through the small opening. She needed to turn so that she was on her belly with her legs hanging down. She then squeezed her body through the window and made sure it was in the same position as when she came in before lowering herself. It allowed her to get her feet onto the top of the stepladder, and she made sure she had her balance before letting go.

She stood in place for only a second before quickly climbing down the stepladder and returning it to the box. The dark shadows of the wall gave her cover as she made her way towards the property entrance. She stood by the large brick post and popped her head to the side to look through the metal bars of the gate. The movement on the opposite side of the street caught her attention and she saw the small figure come out of the shadows and race across to where she was.

"Jenny," a voice hissed.

"Who's there?" she asked.

"It's Carol," the voice replied.

"Do you have a bag?" Jenny went on.

"Yes," Carol answered as her face came in view.

"Get it open then," Jenny instructed her.

Carol did as she was told and Jenny began emptying her pockets and dumping her ill gotten gains in the bag on the other side of the gate.

"This is good stuff," Carol let out as she watched.

"Just get it to Andy as quickly as you can," Jenny said when she finished what she was doing.

She patted down her pockets to make sure everything was out of them before telling Carol to go. It was time to get back to her bedroom and she quickly moved along in the shadow of the wall until she got to the wooden box. A last glance up at the small window showed the building was still dark inside, and it appeared that she'd gotten away with the robbery. Climbing up on the box, she stretched up her arms and just managed to get a grip on the top of the wall. Her muscles ached as she hauled herself up then quickly dropped down to the ground on the other side.

She remained crouched where she was for a few seconds, but all was quiet around her and she raced across the grass to the window she left open. In seconds she was back inside the mansion and she closed the window before making her way to the lobby area. Her heartbeat was racing as she crept down the stairs to the servants' quarters and along to her room. There was one last thing she needed to do, but she quickly changed out of the clothes she was wearing and put on her uniform.

Stepping out of the bedroom again, she sneaked along to the washroom. Once there she filled the basin on the stand with water and cleaned the dirt from her face and hands. She tidied the place after to make sure there was no evidence of what she just did then made her way back to her bedroom. The adrenaline was still flowing when she closed the door and leaned back against it.

The thrill of the robbery made her smile and there was no getting any rest at first when she eventually went to lie down on the bed. It was a while before her heartbeat slowed enough to enable her to calm down, but her mind was in overdrive as the events of the last hour or so continually flashed through it. There was no doubt that Andy would be happy with the haul she got for him that night, and it was a good start in what she hoped was about to be a lucrative few days.

The excitement of the night gradually faded away to be replaced by a growing tiredness, and when Jenny finally closed her eyes, it wasn't long before she was fast asleep.

Chapter 9

The sound of slightly raised voices from the kitchen was a sign that news of the robbery was already out, and Jenny put an impassive expression on her face as she walked inside.

"Sit down, sit down," Jill urged her. "You'll never believe what's happened."

Jenny frowned as she moved to the table and sat down, but she said nothing.

"Tell her what you just told me, Matilda," Jill said.

Jenny turned her attention to the cook.

"Well…" Matilda started. "We were running low on milk, so I went out just after six this morning. When I got to the nearby market, I met one of the maids from next door and she told me that there were problems at the house."

"What sort of problems?" Jenny asked.

"Supposedly some of the owner's possessions went missing last night," Matilda said.

"What?" Jenny exclaimed in feigned surprise. "There was a robbery?"

"That's the strange thing," Matilda said. "According to the maid, there were no signs of a forced entry like you would expect if someone got inside. There were no broken locks or open doors and no smashed windows. She said the master of the house needed to get up early because he is due at a business meeting today and noticed straight away that some of his belongings were missing. But supposedly when he got the butler to check, the house appeared normal."

"That's weird," Jenny said. "What do they think happened?"

Matilda shrugged her shoulders as she went on.

"The maid told me the master of the house ordered that all the rooms of the staff be searched, so maybe he thinks one of his own household is responsible."

"They should get the police in," Jenny replied.

"That's what I said," Matilda replied. "But as far as I know, it hasn't been done yet."

That was good news for Jenny, and she hoped it stayed that way. No police involvement would make it more likely that she wasn't caught.

"Was much stolen?" she asked.

"Some money and some small knickknacks according to the maid," Matilda told her.

Jenny glanced at the clock on the wall to see it was just coming up to seven. She was amazed that news of the crime was already out, but no police involvement yet, and suspicion falling on the staff in the house meant that it was unlikely the theft of the items would be traced back to her. The conversation carried on between Jill and Matilda, but she remained quiet as she ate the breakfast put in front of her by the cook.

When she and Jill finished eating, they got started with their work and things carried on in much the same way as any other day. There was no more news about the robbery when she returned to the kitchen for lunch, and she wasn't sure if that was good or bad. She would have liked to know what was going on, but at the same time didn't want to show too much interest in it.

Usually when she carried out a job for Andy, she was long gone from the scene of the crime before it was discovered, so it seemed strange to be so close to it on this occasion. It was of some concern, but there was nothing she could do but carry on as if everything was normal, and that's what she did that afternoon. The flare of panic was unavoidable when Jill burst into the room she was cleaning at around three, and she couldn't stop the startled expression showing on her face.

"You need to come with me," her work colleague said.

Jenny's pulse rate spiked as the adrenaline returned to her veins.

"Why?" she asked.

"Someone is here and we need to get ready," Jill went on.

Thoughts of the police making enquiries filled Jenny's head.

"What do you mean someone?" she asked.

"A patient," Jill replied. "I was just informed that Mr. Winterbourne agreed to see her this afternoon."

Jenny almost let out a sigh as the panic faded, but managed to stop herself from doing it.

"A patient is here already?" she asked.

"Aren't you listening to me?" Jill complained. "Yes, she's downstairs and we need to get the examination room cleaned, so stop talking and come on."

Jenny's head starting buzzing with thoughts of Thomas Winterbourne administering to a patient, and it was now something else that was making her pulse run fast. She grabbed her equipment and followed Jill out of the room and along the hallway to the set of stairs leading to the examination room. They closed the door when they were inside.

"You mop the floor," Jill said. "I'll clean the table and furniture."

The urgency of the situation was all too apparent to Jenny, but she didn't rush the cleaning of the floor. She wanted Jill to be finished first to see if it got her what she wanted.

"Hurry up," Jill said when she completed the tasks she was doing.

"It's nearly completed," Jenny replied.

"Just get it done quickly," Jill went on. "I'll go down and tell Stevens that the room will be ready in five minutes. When you're finished, just get out of here and keep out of sight in one of the bedrooms."

"Sure," Jenny agreed.

She stood for a second or two when she was alone in the room and contemplated if she could go through with what was on her mind. In the end, the chance to see what went on in the examination room was too much of a temptation for her to resist. Picking up her cleaning equipment, she hurried down the stairs to put it in one of the guest bedrooms. She was supposed to stay there too, but it wasn't what she did. Instead, she left the bedroom and rushed back up the stairs.

When she was in the examination room again, she stepped across to the wardrobe and opened the doors. She moved the boxes in the bottom around to create a small space, so she could conceal herself. What she was doing was crazy and the risk of being caught was real, but she couldn't stop herself. After Maggie first mentioned Thomas Winterbourne's activities as a doctor, she was curious to find out more, and since getting to know him a little, this need became almost insatiable.

She tried to make sure that the boxes and white coats hanging down gave her enough cover, and when she was satisfied that she wouldn't be detected, she closed the wardrobe door and waited. The sound of footsteps entering the examination room a few minutes later made her hold her breath. It was a second or two before she heard her employer's voice.

"If you just take a seat, Mrs. Lambert," Thomas said, "I'll get myself ready."

"Certainly," a feminine voice responded.

There was silence and Jenny froze as the door of the wardrobe opened. It gave her a view of Thomas's crotch and legs and she continued to hold her breath as he selected one of the white coats and took it out. The wardrobe door swung shut again but didn't close all the way.

Jenny let her breath out quietly and tried to hold her nerve. From where she was sitting, she could get a glimpse of the examination table, but she couldn't see either of the people in the room.

"Could you explain your symptoms please?" Thomas said.

"They only started to affect me in the last few months," Mrs. Lambert started.

"Has anything significant changed in your life recently?" Thomas interrupted her.

There was silence for a second, as if she was thinking.

"Nothing of note," she eventually replied.

"And how is the problem manifesting itself?" Thomas asked her.

"I've started to suddenly wake up in a cold sweat in the middle of the night for no reason," Mrs. Lambert went on. "When it happens I have almost uncontrollable shakes and I have irrational fears. Calming my mind is difficult, and it can keep me awake for hours afterwards when it happens."

"These are common symptoms I see regularly," Thomas said. "How often do they occur?"

"It started off infrequently," Mrs. Lambert told him. "But in the last few weeks it has become more regular and it has happened for the last four nights in a row. I'm getting desperate now for a cure and a friend told me that you might be able to provide it."

"Did she tell you anything about how I tackle the problem?" he asked.

"She said it was something about relaxing," Mrs. Lambert replied.

Jenny craned her head to the side to try to get a view of Thomas, but she wasn't able to. She considered trying to ease the door further open, but eventually decided it was too much of a risk. Things were getting interesting and she was aware of how fast her heartbeat was running.

"That's the crux of it," Thomas went on. "I believe there are unknown inhibitions in your life that are creating stress. You need to shed these to help you relax and deal with the problem."

"How do I do that?" Mrs. Lambert asked.

"Well, I believe that massage is the key," Thomas went on. "It can take away the stress and free you of the symptoms you are experiencing. I can offer to show you the best way to do this."

"OK," Mr. Lambert said hesitantly.

"The first thing I must say is that you need to be naked for this therapy," Thomas told her.

"Oh," Mrs. Lambert let out in a shocked tone.

Jenny put her hand over her mouth. She was beginning to understand why it was that Thomas needed to visit a brothel after his therapy sessions with a patient.

"I understand that you may not be comfortable with this," Thomas went on. "But I believe it to be necessary. The studies I've carried out indicate that the massage works better on naked skin. If you'd rather not remove your clothes, then it may be better for you to seek help elsewhere."

"Well…" Mrs. Lambert let out after some further hesitation. "My friend said that her symptoms were eased after you showed her the treatment, so I suppose…"

She didn't finish the sentence, but Jenny guessed that she was about to go through with what was being asked of her. The sexual element of the therapy was unmistakable, and she could barely believe that a refined lady was about to submit to it. The image of her naked on the table under the control of Thomas flashed through her mind and the spark of heat flared between her thighs. It was unexpected and she wanted to squirm, but fear of making a noise made her remain still. The slight shame of her reaction to what was going on blossomed in her mind, but her body seemed to have a will of its own for once and she was a slave to it.

"If you are more comfortable undressing alone, I can leave the room," Thomas said.

"No... no, there is no point in that," Mrs. Lambert said. "You are a professional, so I see no need for you to leave."

"Well, if you can get prepared and lie face down on the table for me please," Thomas went on.

Jenny listened to the sound of Mrs. Lambert getting to her feet and undressing. She found the whole scenario of what was happening strangely arousing, and there was no controlling the flush of arousal she experienced. She tried to ignore it as she kept her eyes on the part of the table she could see out of the wardrobe.

The flash of naked skin made her eyes widen and her gaze settled on a chubby behind when Mrs. Lambert lay down on the table. Jenny was around girls all the time at the gang house and had seen them naked on plenty of occasions when they dressed and undressed. This was different though.

There was a definite sexual charge to the atmosphere and Jenny wondered if the older woman felt it too. It seemed hard to miss and she wondered if Mrs. Lambert was so distressed about her symptoms that she was prepared to go through with whatever was needed to ease them.

"Just remain completely still," Thomas said.

Jenny could just catch a glimpse of him as he began the treatment. She couldn't see quite what he was doing but guessed that he was kneading the naked skin of his patient with his slender fingers. The groan of satisfaction was unexpected and she pressed her hand more firmly across her mouth. There was no doubt that Mrs. Lambert was taking instant enjoyment from what was happening.

Jenny got a clear view of Thomas's hands massaging Mrs. Lambert's naked buttocks then slowly sliding right down to the soles of her feet. He then worked his way back up her body.

"How does that feel?" Thomas asked.

"It's nice and relaxing," Mrs. Lambert let out in a quiet voice.

"I'm working pressure points in your body that should help to relieve your inhibitions and stress," he went on. "The effect should last a while and most patients have found that a few sessions here is enough to rid them of the symptoms they experience. Please now turn over."

Jenny's eyes opened wider as Mrs. Lambert did it without question. She caught a glimpse of neatly trimmed pubic hair and rounded thighs. It was more than obvious now why Thomas got aroused to the point where he needed to seek the help of a working girl in a brothel.

She might be naïve when it came to sex, but even she recognized that what she was witnessing wasn't far short of foreplay. She watched the way his well-manicured fingers caressed across Mrs. Lambert's naked thighs and wondered what was going on in his mind. Was it purely medical thoughts that he was having? It was unlikely considering that the therapy got him erect, and her suspicions were that his inability to control himself and the fact that he got sexual pleasure from the treatment was shameful to him.

It was what she was feeling herself as she watched. Her panties were getting damp and the urge to squirm was more acute now. It needed all of her willpower to remain still as she kept her gaze on what was going on until it ended. She could hear the heavy breathing of Mrs. Lambert and there was no doubt the older woman was relaxed.

"That's your first session over," Thomas said. "What I need you to do now is see what happens when you sleep tonight. Hopefully you won't experience any problems, but it usually requires a few sessions to get real results. If you come back on the same day next week, we can continue."

The patient seemed in no hurry to get back to her feet, but she eventually did and disappeared out of sight. Jenny listened to the sound of clothes being put back on.

"Thank you," Mrs. Lambert said.

"My butler should be at the bottom of the stairs when you leave the room," Thomas told her. "He will escort you out and I'll see you next week."

Jenny heard the sound of Mrs. Lambert leaving followed by footsteps coming across the room. She froze in position as the door of the wardrobe opened to the sight of the white coat. Thomas loosened the buttons to remove it and she found herself staring at his crotch again. The hard bulge showed the evidence of his intense sexual arousal and she couldn't take her eyes from it.

He hung up the white coat and remained standing in place as he tried to calm himself. The bulge gradually faded away as he got control of his body, but Jenny knew that it was only temporary. If Maggie was right, the man she was spying on would be making a trip to The Teahouse brothel that afternoon and one of the girls there would play out the game of being his patient then get her hands on his erection to release the pent up desire.

The unexpected wish that the girl was her flashed through Jenny's mind and surprised her. Apart from the couple of curious fumbled experiments with boys, sex was something that happened in the lives of other people, but here she was fantasizing about it. Her eyes remained on Thomas's crotch until he closed the wardrobe door and she heard the sound of his footsteps crossing the room as he left.

She remained where she was for a few minutes more to make sure he didn't come back before getting to her feet. Opening the door of the wardrobe, she stepped out and closed it again. She hurried to leave the room then made her way downstairs and back in the bedroom where she left her cleaning equipment. It was impossible to get her mind from what she just saw, and the arousal it brought on while she was hiding in the examination room refused to die down.

Jenny picked up her equipment and moved back to the room she was cleaning when Jill first interrupted her. She tried to get on with the work she needed to do, but she couldn't take her attention from the prickle of heat between her thighs. It was driving her crazy like never before and the images of Thomas's svelte, almost graceful fingers massaging naked skin wouldn't leave her mind.

She walked to the door of the bedroom and opened it to listen. It reminded her of being in the neighboring property the night before, when the fear of being caught in the midst of a robbery made her pulse race fast. She was experiencing a similar sensation at that very moment, but it was caused by something altogether different. The hallway was quiet, so she closed the door and moved back across the room to the bed.

"This is crazy," she muttered, but she needed to do something to take away the burning arousal that was raging through her body.

She dropped on the mattress and lifted her butt to drag her uniform up around her waist. Her mind was on what she just witnessed as she spread her legs and slid a hand in between. It was the first occasion in a long while that she experienced such an unbridled rush of libido, and shame mixed with concern in her mind that she wasn't in control of herself. It wasn't long before she didn't care. All that mattered was the pleasure she could give herself and there was no stopping.

She closed her eyes and imagined it was Thomas's fingertips stroking on the wet material of her underwear. The touch made her gasp and she bit her lip to stop herself from making a louder noise. Her fingers were soaked in seconds as her body responded, and she knew that she was going to do more than just play with herself through her panties. She raised her hips up so that she could drag the white material partway down her thighs.

A shiver rippled down her spine when she touched on naked skin and her body arched up from the mattress as the firm, circular motion of her fingertips exposed slick pink skin. She bit her lip harder as the urge to groan became almost overwhelming and she couldn't stop her body bucking around as her fingertips grazed roughly over her clitoris. Her head pressed back against the mattress as she teased the erect bud, and it was impossible to stop her breath rushing out.

Her mind was filled with images of the scene in the examination room. In truth she only got a glimpse of it, but that was enough to bring out a sexual drive that was setting her body alight. Jenny closed her lips tightly together as she slid her hand lower until her fingers were poised at her slick pussy entrance.

"This is crazy," she repeated then ignored the words straight away as she slid her fingers inside.

It stretched her tight, virgin pussy and made her buck up again. The fantasy coming to life was that Thomas's fingers were plunging deeper inside her quivering cunt, and that stoked her desire even more. She imagined the thrill of him giving her one of his medical massages as she circled her fingers in her slick hole then began to stroke them in and out. The idea that it was her getting him erect only heightened her excitement and her breathing grew ever more ragged as she finger fucked herself. The growing pressure made her speed up the rhythm until she was driving her touch in frantically to take herself all the way.

The fantasy in her head moved on to her helping Thomas and she started to lose control. She continued to thrust her fingers all the way inside until she was almost there, and then she brought them out and rubbed her clit furiously. Her hips lifted up from the bed until her back was arched tightly and she remained in that position until the tension broke. A violent shudder sent her crashing back to the mattress and the burst of raw pleasure erupted through her petite frame. She squeezed her legs tightly together as the hot spasms between her thighs rocked her body. They grew stronger as she climbed the heights of her passion before the trembling shudders began to die away as the calm slowly returned.

It was a couple of minutes before she was able to summon the energy to make a move, and she grabbed her panties to drag them back in place. Quickly moving to the edge of the bed, she got to her feet and was all too aware how badly her legs were trembling. Her uniform slid back down from around her waist and she smoothed the covers to remove any evidence that she was ever on the bed.

It would be a more difficult job to erase from her mind what she just did and why she did it. Images from the examination room still flashed through her head and she was unable to shrug them off. She'd come into Thomas Winterbourne's home expecting to hate him and happily relieve him of his prized possessions. That certainly wasn't what she was thinking about him when she was lying on the bed.

"This is not good," Jenny let out in a breathless voice.

Things were getting out of hand and she wasn't sure she could cope.

Chapter 10

"Get off me woman, will you?" Andy complained.

Maggie ignored his protests to keep hugging him and enjoyed his muscular chest crushing against her breasts as she kept a tight hold on him. There was no doubt the touch of her voluptuous curves was having an effect and the slight stirrings of an erection coming to life were unmistakable. When she finally released her grip and backed off, she flicked her gaze to Andy's crotch, although her attention quickly turned to the money in her hand. It was more than she ever expected.

"I can't believe you're giving it to me," she let out.

"It's what we agreed for you bringing the plan to me," Andy replied. "You get ten percent of whatever we take."

"I know, but…" Maggie started then didn't know quite how to go on. She looked up and almost let out a laugh as he moved away. "Don't worry," she teased him. "I'm not going to hug you again."

"I'm not worried," he let out, but his slight embarrassment at her show of affection and his reaction to it was evident as he fiddled with his hat then brushed away some imaginary dust from the front of his suit.

"These properties are well worth targeting then?" Maggie said.

"What do you think?" Andy replied. "The owners are obviously rich and going by Jenny's first haul, we are going to do very well out of this."

Maggie looked down at her share of the proceeds and a smile broke out on her face. She was already making plans for a trip to the hairdresser to get a red rinse and she would follow that up by shopping for some new finery to wear. That was for another day, however, and she sat back down at the table in The Teahouse.

"Do you think Jenny will get here tonight?" she asked.

"Monday evening was the agreement for the next meeting, so I'm sure she'll come if she can," Andy answered. "I guess it will all depend on whether she can get away from her duties."

He glanced across at the clock on the wall and saw it was already after six. There was nothing he could do but sit down to wait, and he chatted with Maggie as the minutes ticked by towards seven. They looked expectantly at the door whenever it opened, but on each occasion it was to the sight of a customer coming in.

"He was here again," Maggie let out at one point.

Andy's brow creased as he looked at her and she could see he didn't understand what she was talking about.

"Who was?" he asked.

"Thomas Winterbourne," Maggie went on. "I'm guessing that he saw a patient on Saturday afternoon because he turned up here in the early evening."

"One of the girls gave him what he wanted then, I take it," Andy went on with a grin.

"Yeah," Maggie replied and said no more.

She wasn't about to admit that she was the one on the receiving end of Thomas Winterbourne's lust. Not that she was ashamed of what she did. She got just as much pleasure from the arrangement as the man she serviced. The touch of his fingers easily brought her to an orgasm and she'd always been thrilled at making a man lose control. She wasn't going to confess that to Andy. Her hope was still that something would eventually happen between them, and she wasn't about to say anything that might jeopardize that.

"Maybe she couldn't get away," he commented.

She glanced at him and thoughts of her encounter with Thomas in the brothel faded. It was now after seven and she nodded her head.

"What do we do…" she started to ask, but the sound of the door opening again stopped her words.

She was expecting to deal with another customer, but immediately saw that wasn't the case as she caught sight of the petite figure of Jenny. Mrs. Harper complained as usual when she was made to take over at the table, but Maggie gave her a couple of coins to keep her quiet. She led the way to the room on the ground floor and they sat down around the table.

"Did you have problems getting away today?" Andy asked.

"No, not really," Jenny replied. "There was just some work I needed to get finished before I asked to leave."

"How is the master of the house treating you?" Andy asked.

"Fine," Jenny answered in a flat voice and shrugged her shoulders.

"Are you OK?" Andy went on.

"I'm fine," Jenny answered in a slightly irritated tone.

Andy glanced across at Maggie, who gave a quick shrug of her shoulders. It was obvious that Jenny was subdued, but there could be any number of reasons for that.

"So… what other opportunities have you spotted?" Andy asked.

"None really," Jenny answered. "There was a lot of fuss about the robbery on Friday, so I just kept my head down and stuck to being a maid."

There was some truth to what she was saying. She'd found out through Matilda that the police were eventually brought in by the owners of the next door property, but as far as she knew suspicion still fell on the staff. Even if that was the case, it seemed like a good idea to just keep a low profile and get on with her work.

In reality, it was the events of Saturday afternoon in the examination room that weighed more heavily on her mind. They sparked something in her that had lain dormant, and she couldn't deny the feelings she was having for the man she worked for. A glimpse of him was enough to bring them out, and it was leaving her in a quandary. She was there to steal from him and knew that Andy would ask her to go through with it at some point, but for once she found herself not really wanting to do it.

The misgivings she was experiencing were alien to her, and she didn't really like having them. She'd never really felt any sympathy for the victims of her crimes, and if anything took a cruel delight in stealing from the well-to-do people Andy targeted. That wasn't the case with Thomas Winterbourne, and a connection was developing between them that was going to make things difficult.

"So you have no idea what you are going to do next?" Andy asked.

Jenny slowly shook her head.

"Not yet anyway," she said. "I just need to wait and see what opportunities appear."

She kept her gaze on the table but was all too aware of the way Andy was staring at her and wondered if he suspected anything.

"Are you sure you're OK?" he asked.

"Yes," Jenny let out then realized how exasperated her response was. "Look…" she went on, "the police were called in to the next property and it's making me nervous to be so close to it."

"Maybe you should just get out then," Andy replied.

"What?" Jenny and Maggie exclaimed at the same time.

Andy got to his feet to pace back and forth.

"We made a good bit of money from what you stole the other night," he went on. "It's no surprise that the police are sniffing around. Maybe we just need to target that box of jewelry and get you out of there."

"Wait," Maggie said. "If she disappears that might lead them back to the Colwell Agency and the fact that I put pressure on the manager to get her the job."

"So, we just let him know that if anything comes back to you that his wife will find out about his activities in a brothel," Andy said. "That should keep him quiet."

"I don't know," Maggie let out.

"What about the other residences in the area?" Jenny said. "Don't you want to target them?"

"Ideally, yes," he replied. "But if too many get hit, then the police are really going to come down hard. I would say take a couple of days to see if you spot any decent opportunities. We can go back and target those properties at a later date. For the moment you just get that jewelry and get out. The money we make from that should be more than enough to tide us over for a long time."

"I'm not sure," Jenny said.

"You're not going soft on me here, are you?" Andy asked when he sat down again and stared across the table.

"No," she exclaimed and was aware of how defensive she sounded. "I think we might just be missing out on some good opportunities."

"Maybe," Andy said. "But like I say, if you spot anything decent, we can always go back at a later date when the heat has died down. Right now the opportunity I don't want to miss is that box of expensive trinkets in Winterbourne's bedroom. For all we know, a few more robberies in the area might spook him into putting them somewhere a lot safer where we can't get to them. I think the smart thing is for you to steal them and take your leave of the property. You can come home or maybe even take a trip somewhere for a few months."

Jenny said nothing and just stared at the table. She'd protested when she was first told that they wanted her to go in the mansion as a maid. Now the thought in her mind was that she wanted to protest about being told to leave. She couldn't admit that and just sat silently.

"The money we make from this could set us up, Jenny," Andy urged her. "So just go get it done as soon as you can."

She was still quiet as her mind ticked over.

"Jenny?" Andy queried to get a response.

"Yeah, OK, OK," she snapped as she got up. "I'll do it."

Her sudden show of petulance was ignored.

"Good girl," Andy said. "When you have the jewelry just come back home. We'll sort everything else out from there."

"Sure," Jenny agreed and walked to the door to leave before the other two got to their feet.

"That was strange," Maggie commented when she and Andy stood up.

"Yeah, but it can't be easy for her in that mansion," he replied. "You know how much she detests the upper classes. Maybe the stress of it all is just getting to her, and it's best that she gets out."

"Maybe," Maggie replied, but she sensed something else was going on and intuition told her that Jenny's behavior that evening was about more than just the stress of a robbery.

Chapter 11

"You're very quiet today, child," Matilda said as she put the breakfast plate and cup down on the table.

"I'm just a bit tired," Jenny lied.

"You must have been tired for the last couple of days then," the cook teased her. "You've hardly said a word."

"Things on my mind," Jenny replied and picked up the cup to take a sip of tea before starting to eat the food on the plate.

Her second comment of the morning was no lie. Since the meeting in The Teahouse two days previously, she'd been going over and over what she should do. She knew her loyalty should be to Andy, the gang and the others they looked after, but for once it wasn't that simple. Her budding attraction to and feelings for Thomas Winterbourne brought out her guilt that she was deceiving him with an act of being a good employee, when in fact her real reason for being in his home was to fleece him of his belongings.

It was making her question if she should actually go through with the plan to rob him, but if she didn't that would put her in an impossible position with Andy. She owed him everything for the help he gave her and the idea of letting him down didn't bear thinking about. It was eating her up trying to decide what she should do, and that was the reason she'd been quiet. As she pondered the problem yet again, she let out a resigned sigh that she immediately knew was too loud and saw Matilda glance towards her. The cook looked as if she was about to ask something, but luckily Jill came in the kitchen at that very second and the question never came.

"You're up early," her fellow maid said when she sat at the table.

"Keen to get going," Jenny replied and forced a smile onto her face.

"Don't let me stop you," Jill shot back and laughed.

Jenny finished her tea then got to her feet. She picked up the cup and plate to take them over to the large sink.

"I was only joking," Jill went on.

"I might as well just get started in the dining room," Jenny said.

She went to the storeroom to get the gear she needed then walked out of the kitchen without saying any more. The cleaning in the dining room was already finished when Jill caught up, and the pair of them then worked together to get what was needed to set the table. Afterwards they moved to the study to get it cleaned and ready for their boss before moving on to other work.

Jenny was glad when they went their separate ways. Chatting with Jill grated on her nerves and she really wasn't in the mood for it. The quiet of being on her own gave her a chance to think, although that didn't really get her anywhere. She knew that she needed to make a decision one way or the other before too long, as there was no way she could just carry on as she was. If she committed to Andy and the gang by going through with the plan, that would mean forgetting about Thomas and giving up on an opportunity she wasn't sure she wanted to miss out on. The alternative was to find out if the spark of whatever it was between the two of them led on to something more, but that would take time she didn't really have.

Throughout that day she weighed the pros and cons of each without actually coming anywhere near to choosing one or the other. She was torn between her allegiance to the gang and her attraction to Thomas, and it turned out to be the smallest of things that finally made her mind up. She finished her work on the first floor at just before six and left the room she'd been working in to return to the servants' quarters. The voices came to her before she reached the stairs leading down to the ground floor and she stopped to watch.

Thomas was talking to Jill in the lobby area and the cigar in his hand revealed that he was probably about to go to the front of the house to relax. There was nothing particularly startling to the exchange she observed and she could barely hear what was being said, but it was clear to her it was master and servant. It brought it home to her that the two people speaking were worlds apart, and while they might be in the same house, they lived different lives.

She wasn't even a maid. It was simply a lie to get her in the house, and her real life as a common thief made it even less likely that she would be welcomed into the circles that Thomas moved in. She continued watching until the conversation ended and Jill headed in the direction of the study while Thomas moved towards the front door of the property. In a flash her mind was made up and she turned to move back along the hallway. The chance was there to take the jewelry then leave the premises that evening before Thomas went to bed. Her heartbeat began to race as she reached his bedroom and she hesitated with her hand on the doorknob. She stopped for only an instant to look back along the hallway, and when she saw it was deserted, she opened the door and walked inside.

Her nerves were jangling as she stepped across the room to where the ornate box was sitting on the dressing table. She was suddenly concerned that Thomas might have secreted the contents elsewhere in the house because of the robbery in the neighboring property, but she lifted the lid to the sight of the pretty jewelry still sitting inside. She picked up the pearl necklace and held it against her neck as she stared at herself in the mirror.

"Some chance of you ever owning something like that," she muttered and placed the necklace in the pocket of her uniform.

She was quick to start grabbing the rest of the pieces and was so consumed with what she was doing that the quiet click of the door opening passed her by. It was only when she looked at herself in the mirror that she became aware that she wasn't alone in the bedroom any more. She didn't miss the sound of the door closing and spun around. The shock registered on her face as she saw Thomas blocking her escape from the room, and she knew there was no point in trying to deny anything. She'd been caught red handed.

"What the hell do you think you're doing, Jenny?" he demanded in a harsh voice.

She'd expected him to shout for someone or completely lose his temper, but it was controlled fury she saw on his face as she stared at him.

"Mr. Winterbourne, I'm…" she started but was cut off.

"You're stealing from me," he interrupted in a jarring tone.

Jenny dropped her gaze to the floor as she frantically tried to come up with an excuse, but she knew it was useless. Her gaze settled on the unlit cigar that Thomas dropped and she couldn't look away from it.

"Have you got nothing to say?" he let out as he stepped away from the door and moved towards her.

There was only one thing Jenny could think of that might get her out of the perilous situation she was now in, but she also knew that it might make matters worse for her. She didn't get the chance to say anything as Thomas went on talking.

"Maybe you'd prefer explaining to the police why you are in my bedroom with your pocket full of my grandmother's treasured belongings?" Thomas went on in an angry voice.

The threat made Jenny act.

"You can have me," she said.

"I can what?" Thomas demanded.

She turned and emptied the jewelry from her pocket back into the box before facing him again.

"I know what you do in your examination room," she said. "And I know the way it makes you feel."

She saw the slight hesitation as he stopped moving and she jumped on it.

"I swear this won't ever happen again," she went on. "If you promise not to involve the police, I'll let you have me in your examination room. You can treat me like a patient to start with, but then you're free to play out the fantasies you have on me. If you want me out of here at the end of it, then I'll walk away and you won't ever see me again."

She held her breath as she waited for the explosion of anger, but her hopes rose when it didn't come. Thomas narrowed his eyes as he glared at her, but the silence stretched out.

"How do you know what I do in my examination room?" he eventually asked.

Jenny took heart from the question. It was a sign that he might actually consider taking her up on the offer, but she wasn't about to confess to him the full reason she knew about his activities.

"I was rushing to clean the room on Saturday but wasn't finished when I heard you coming up the stairs," Jenny said. "I thought you might be mad that I was still there, so I hid in the wardrobe. I heard you giving the massage to Mrs. Lambert."

"You were spying on me," he accused her.

It was the truth, but again she wasn't about to admit that. Her mouth was now moving faster than her brain and she was speaking without really thinking in an attempt to wriggle out of a dangerous situation.

"No," she exclaimed. "I just got trapped in the room and panicked. I saw you put on the white coat then heard everything as you gave your patient her treatment. When you removed the white coat afterwards, I saw... well, I saw how you reacted."

Her breathing was shallow as she stopped talking. She waited for Thomas to say something, but when he didn't she went on.

"It must be frustrating for you to have fantasies about your patients that get you in such a state and not have an outlet for it." She paused for a second or two before making the offer again. "You can have it with me," she told him. "You can do whatever you want as long as I don't get in trouble."

"Did you steal from the house next door?" he asked.

"No," she lied. "But it gave me the idea to try and steal from you. I'm really sorry."

She could see he was weighing up his options as the silence surrounded them again. A glance at his crotch showed a hint of the bulge she saw on Saturday and she moved closer to him.

"I promise you can use me however you want," she told him.

"Turn out your pocket," he ordered her.

Jenny did it to show that she'd put everything back in the box and it was now down to Thomas. If he was able to resist his desires, then she was in serious trouble and she closed her eyes as she waited for him to say something. It was actions, not words that made her eyelids snap back open. The grip on her wrist was tight and she gasped as she was led across to the door.

"Check if there's anyone out there," Thomas ordered her.

It was more than just the shock of being caught that was making her heartbeat hammer in her chest now. Her offer was accepted and the flare of exhilaration was intense. She reached for the handle and turned it to edge the door open enough to stick her head out and hurriedly glance both ways. The hallway was as deserted as it was before she came in the room and she ducked back inside.

"It's empty," she said in a hushed voice.

The grip returned to her wrist and that touch was enough to send her pulse racing faster still. She was about to give herself to a man and only half knew what she was getting into. If Thomas played out his fantasy of her being a patient, then she would be naked on the examination table with his fingers kneading her body. She saw that much for herself on Saturday when he dealt with an actual patient. The thought of what might happen after the massage ended scared and excited her, but she knew for sure there was no getting away from it.

They stepped out of the bedroom and closed the door before she was led along to the stairs at the end of the hallway. Her mind was in turmoil. Only minutes before she was on the verge of stealing Thomas's belongings and fleeing the house. Now she was his sexual plaything and she was amazed at her own longing for what was about to take place. The emotions assailing her were intense and her breathing was ragged even before she was briskly made to climb the stairs and enter the examination room.

She halted when she saw the table and tried to shake off the grip on her wrist. It tightened to haul her to the center of the room and only then did Thomas let go. The lust shone in his eyes as they faced each other and she wasn't sure if it was for her or the situation she was giving him.

"You were here on Saturday," he said. "You know what to do."

He turned away to walk to the wardrobe and she watched as he opened it to take out a white coat. She was still standing immobile after he put it on and came back. He stepped right up to her and cupped her chin to make her look up. His powerful body towered over her petite frame and a shiver rippled down her spine.

"You need to be naked for the treatment," he said quietly.

"Yes, sir," she replied as she stepped back.

She closed her eyes but knew that his gaze remained on her as she reached for the hem of her uniform and eased it up her body. Her nerves sprung up more than ever at revealing herself to him, but there was no backing out. The truth was that she didn't want to, but the closer she got to submitting completely to him, the more she realized just what it was she was getting herself into.

Jenny worked the uniform over her head then simply dropped it on the floor. Her chest heaved as gasping breaths spilled out and her hands were trembling as she reached for the hook of her bra. When it was loosened, she held an arm across her chest as she nudged the straps from her shoulders.

"Don't keep me waiting," Thomas urged her.

The sound of his voice made her open her eyes again and she saw his intense gaze as she did as she was told. Pulling her arm away let the bra slide down to expose her breasts, and she saw Thomas unconsciously lick his lips as he enjoyed the sight of her half naked body. It made her shudder as she let the bra drop to the floor.

"Now the panties," Thomas instructed her.

Jenny could already make out the dampness on the material and there was slight shame that the humiliating ordeal was bringing out an arousal that she couldn't contain. Her hands shook even more as she touched her fingers on her hips then worked them below the white material. She kept her legs together as she eased her panties down to step out of them then straightened up again. Her head was bowed as she stared at the floor and she kept her hands in front of her thighs to cover herself.

"Get on the table face down," Thomas ordered.

The hoarse pitch to his voice was all too evident, and it revealed his own excitement at being in charge of a patient that was going to let him do more than just massage her. Jenny tried to retain some of her modesty as she stepped over to the table and got on it. She shuffled around to try and get herself comfortable, but she was too tense. The touch of Thomas's hands on her shoulders made her gasp, and she trembled as his slender fingers sank into her naked skin. She squeezed her legs tightly together and was all too aware of the slick sensation on her thighs as the massage got underway.

There was a growing tension as Thomas's fingers slid down her spine and continued to dig into her flesh. She couldn't stop herself squirming as they reached her lower back. Up to that point it appeared that she was being given a treatment, but that ended when a single finger slid along the crease of her butt. The tingling sensation made her groan and she pressed her face against the leather table to stifle the sound.

She heard his quiet laugh and tried to control herself, but the touch of his finger stroking on her soft skin again made her wriggle around. The sensation ended as he groped her rounded buttocks before working his hands all the way down her legs to her feet. The touch immediately came back up again, but this time she was aware of his fingers forcing between her thighs. She instinctively squeezed her legs tighter together, but it was no protection.

Her groan was louder as Thomas's fingers explored more intimately. The shudders wracking her body grew stronger and there was no resisting the powerful grip that spread her legs apart. She closed her eyes as fingers stroked along her swollen lips. The flood of heat erupted to make her thighs spasm, but the touch then moved higher again to run up her spine to the nape of her neck. Her hair was swept aside and she couldn't hold in the rush of breath as fingertips caressed across her sensitive skin. She shuddered as warm breath played on her ear and knew he was leaning down. His lips didn't quite press on her, but she heard his quiet whisper.

"Turn over, little girl."

Jenny hesitated for only an instant before she rolled onto her back. She was showing him everything, but her eyes were closed. It meant she didn't see his hands coming, and the expected touch on her shoulders to continue the massage didn't happen. Instead, fingertips brushed across a nipple and the hot flood of pleasure made her back arch up from the surface of the table. It brought out another quiet laugh from Thomas and she knew he was toying with her.

Her nipple stiffened and she groaned as it was tweaked. The slight pain faded as Thomas's fingertips circled gently on the soft skin around her erect bud.

The touch trailed to her cleavage and stroked along it before sliding to her other nipple. The teasing was already driving her crazy and things were hardly even started. It was setting her body alight and the tingling on her skin grew stronger as her breasts were groped.

She kept her legs slightly apart on this occasion when the massage slid lower. The muscles of her midriff fluttered to make her squirm, and it made her crave Thomas's touch between her thighs. The sweat began to prickle on her skin as it came closer, but she groaned as his fingers slid along the front of her thighs and kneaded her legs on the way down to her feet. She wanted to beg him for more, but her embarrassment swelled at the thought of acting so wantonly and she remained silent.

Her virgin body was responding to the erotic massage to make her wetter still, and she couldn't stop her mind turning to just how hard Thomas was. It was impossible to see with the white coat blocking her view, but she suspected he would already be fully erect. He was living his fantasy and likely doing to her the things he visualized when he was treating a patient. For once his perversions weren't stifled and there was no doubt his lust was coming out.

Jenny gasped as the grip of his hands tightened around her ankles and suddenly she was squealing and grasping for the sides of the table as she was dragged down it. Her feet and legs spilled over the bottom to hang towards the floor, and it left her perched with her ass right on the edge. She lifted her head as her legs were pushed apart and watched as Thomas dropped to his knees between them. The warmth of his breath played on her skin again, but on this occasion she got more than just that and bit her lips as the kiss pressed between her thighs.

"Oh god," she let out in an almost despairing sounding voice.

"You like it when boys kiss you like that?" Thomas asked.

"First time," gasped Jenny.

"You're untouched," he went on.

"Yes," admitted Jenny.

The kiss pressed harder on her skin and she guessed that Thomas was excited by her confession. That he was getting to live his fantasy with a virgin brought out a stronger lust in him, and Jenny's toes curled as his tongue came out to sweep along her wet slit. Every muscle in her body tensed to make her buttocks clench and her back arched as the hot bliss erupted to life between her thighs. The short stubble on Thomas's jaw prickled against her thighs to make the sweet sensation even more delicious and she was lost to the moment. His tongue teased her wet entrance to dip just inside and she bit her lip to hold in the cry that threatened to burst out. The rough touch of fingers pressed on her slick skin to open her wider and it allowed his tongue to plunge deeper.

Jenny finally couldn't hold in the groan as her excitement mounted. She remembered masturbating on the bed as she fantasized about Thomas, but what was happening was so much better than that and she wriggled and writhed on the table top as his tongue probed her depths and swept across her slick inner skin with rasping licks. Her groan was louder when his tongue came back out, and she was sure he was about to take her virginity when he got to his feet and removed the white coat. She saw the way his solid erection strained at the front of his pants and shuddered at the thought she was about to see it.

It didn't happen, however, and Thomas stepped from between her thighs and moved around the examination table. It appeared the game was only just starting and that she was about to be on the receiving end of more of his perversions. That she wanted to be exactly where she was didn't come as a complete surprise, but her nerves still spiked when her wrists were grabbed to pull her legs back onto the table. It left her stretched out on her back and wondering what was about to happen.

Her dark hair fell across her eyes as she turned her head, and Thomas reached out to brush it back from her forehead. She stared up at him and their eyes locked together for a few seconds. The connection she felt when she almost bumped into him the first time they met was there again, and she was sure that he was aware of it too.

"You shouldn't have tried to steal from me," he chastised her.

"But it got you something you wanted," she replied.

The smile slowly spread across his face.

"That's true," he said. "But you still need to be punished, so roll over."

"But..." Jenny started.

"Roll over," he snapped. "You said you would do whatever I wanted, so don't try and get out of it now."

Jenny was shaking as she complied. She closed her eyes as her right arm was stretched out towards a strap and in seconds it was secured around her wrist. Her left arm was strapped in place too, and it left her lying face down on the table and unable to escape. She expected her feet to be tied down as well, but it didn't happen and she shuddered as her hair was brushed aside to expose the nape of her neck.

"You have a pretty body," Thomas commented. "I noticed that when I first saw you."

Jenny said nothing and just pressed her face against the leather as his fingertips grazed seductively across her sensitive skin. Her breathing became ragged almost straight away as the touch slid from her neck to her spine. It slowly traced all the way down until the tingling sensation made her buttocks clench as Thomas stroked along the crease of her butt. It was a sensual torment that was igniting her desire for more, but as her employer's palm clapped down on her buttocks, she knew that it was pain she was about to endure.

"Are you going to try and steal from me again?" Thomas asked.

"I promise with all my heart that I won't," Jenny replied.

What she was saying was true, but it was also an attempt to get out of the punishment she was sure was coming her way. She bit her lip as Thomas's hand lifted from her butt and tried to prepare herself. His palm came down with more power now and her body bucked as the painful spank assailed her.

"Please," she begged in a breathless voice. "I give you my word I won't steal from you."

"Not good enough," he snapped. "You need to learn the hard way."

The flare of agony erupted again as Thomas's hand cracked down on reddened skin and Jenny clenched her buttocks in anticipation of more. It was no protection against the hot pain and she strained against the straps around her wrist as she was chastised. Her chest heaved against the leather as it continued and she let out a long breath only when the punishing onslaught ended.

"You understand that you belong to me now, don't you?" Thomas said.

"Yes," Jenny let out.

The words thrilled her like she couldn't believe. She wasn't quite sure how she would fit into Thomas's life, but she wanted to be his more than anything. Her groan came out as his fingertips stroked down between her thighs to turn the searing hurt of punishment to the burning pleasure of arousal.

"Does that feel good?' he asked.

"Yes," Jenny replied between gasps.

"Do you masturbate?" he demanded to know.

The flush of embarrassment reddened Jenny's face as she remembered doing just that after witnessing Thomas treating a patient on Saturday. For once she didn't lie to him.

"Yes," she confessed.

"So you recognize the signs of when you're about to orgasm?" he went on.

Jenny trembled as his fingers stroked along her pussy. She just managed to get the answer out to tell him yes through more gasping breaths when the touch between her thighs grew rougher. Thomas's fingers began wriggling around at her pussy entrance and she pressed her face against the leather of the table as the penetration stretched her open. The sensation of stiff, slender fingers fucking into her tight, wet cunt was something special and her body began to shake.

Things got better still when Thomas leaned down to kiss on her butt and his tongue flicked out to lick along the crease of her ass. She could hear his heavy breathing as he indulged in the perversions he'd only showed to prostitutes before and they were setting Jenny's body alight. The rush of pure delight flooded her veins as his fingers began to stroke in and out of her pussy and the climb towards a climax gained momentum.

Thomas forced his tongue between her soft, rounded cheeks and the shame that she was letting him touch her in such a way welled up in Jenny's mind. That she wanted it made the humiliation all the more acute, but she writhed around as the pure bliss of his tongue rasping over her puckered skin came alive. She strained against the straps securing her wrists in place, but she couldn't escape even if she wanted to as the exquisite torment continued.

Thomas lifted his head as he worked to slide his fingers in Jenny's slick pussy with an even faster rhythm. It was making her lose control and she found herself desperate for a climax to release the pressure in her body.

"Tell me when you're going to cum," Thomas ordered as he increased his efforts to get her there.

The tension in Jenny's body built towards a peak and in seconds she was right on the cusp of an orgasm and ready to enjoy it.

"I'm there," she said.

She groaned as Thomas pulled his fingers out and left her teetering right on the edge. It was torture to be taken so close and then denied what she wanted, and she struggled against the bonds holding her to the table.

"Please," she cried out desperately.

It only got her the soft laugh of Thomas as he moved up the side of the table and stroked her hair.

"Free my hands," Jenny let out, but she knew it wasn't going to happen.

Without the touch between her thighs, the heat of arousal receded and she was going to have to wait.

"You cum when I say you cum," Thomas teased her.

She gasped for breath as the bonds were released, but it was only to allow her to roll onto her back. As soon as she was in place, her wrists were strapped down again. When Thomas finished, he moved to the foot of the table and Jenny could do nothing as her legs were spread wide apart. The straps were wound around her ankles and clasped in place to leave her tied down and completely at the mercy of the man having his fun with her.

He moved into position so that he was staring down at her face, and Jenny lay completely still as he leaned down. The kiss was gentle to begin with, but Thomas's lust came out as their lips pressed together more intensely. Jenny rocked her head from side to side when the kiss ended and her dark hair fell across her face.

"Too pretty to hide," Thomas said with a smile as he brushed it away.

His hand caressed her cheek as he leaned down to another kiss. It was over quickly and Jenny gasped as his lips began to move down her body. She groaned when he got to her upper chest and flicked out his tongue to lick a wet trail down to her cleavage. The touch moved onto a breast and circled around her stiff nipple. Her back arched when Thomas wrapped his lips around the erect bud to take it in his mouth. He sucked hard on it and Jenny squirmed as her arousal flared again.

The desperation for an orgasm returned to her mind, but she was tied down to the table and had absolutely no say in when or even if she got it. Thomas was completely in control and playing out his fantasies and there was no knowing what that involved. His lips tightened around her nipple as he sucked it deeper in his mouth and the tension returned to her body. The climb towards a climax erupted to life again and all she could hope was that this time she wasn't denied it.

The pressure eased around her nipple when Thomas released it from his mouth, but only so he could kiss across her chest to tease and torment the other one. His head moved back and forth to take what he wanted before he began kissing lower. Jenny's body twitched and convulsed as the soft caress of lips slid across her belly then between her thighs. She closed her eyes tightly and forced her head back against the leather as she got the touch she wanted.

Thomas was bringing out a wanton side to her nature that she didn't even know she possessed, but she wanted to please him and do whatever he desired so she could be his. Her arms and legs flexed to strain against the straps holding her down as the kisses between her thighs made the arousal blossom more.

Her neck stretched out as she pressed her head back and waited for the penetration. It was something even better that she got and she squealed as a rough lick rasped across her clit.

Suddenly she was struggling to get her breath out as her excitement mounted. The licking on her clit continued as Thomas's fingers stroked around her slick entrance and slowly but surely she was stretched open again. She began to thrash around as the erotic onslaught continued, and it drove her closer and closer to the moment she wanted.

Eager fingers pumped in and out of her virgin pussy as Thomas swept his tongue over her erect clit again and again. Her butt lifted from the table as the tension gripped her muscles and in a matter of seconds she was braced on the very edge of losing control. She said nothing, but her desperate breaths were a sign that she was on the cusp of an orgasm. The pleasure didn't stop on this occasion, and her lover seemed completely caught up in his lust. The pressure boiled over to send her crashing back to the table and Jenny let out a cry as she was engulfed in the hot bliss of a climax.

Thomas drove his fingers deep and the spasms of Jenny's pussy rippled around the stiff penetration. The hot flood of ecstasy ripped through her to take her higher until she was ultimately lost to the peak of her passion. Strong convulsions rocked her body as Thomas continued to lick on her clit to string the pleasure out for as long as possible, and she was only released from the shuddering delight of the climax when he moved back.

She groaned as his fingers withdrew and he was quick to move up the side of the table and start releasing the strap around her right wrist. She remembered Maggie's words that the action in the brothel ended with the girl jacking him off and realized what he was doing.

"No," she let out in a gasping voice. "I belong to you. Take my virginity."

Thomas stopped what he was doing and stared at her. His hunger for her flashed in his eyes as she nodded her head, and the nervousness ripped through her as he started to rip the clothes from his body. She couldn't take her eyes from the sight and watched as his muscular chest came in view. He threw his shirt to the floor and unbuttoned his pants.

Jenny saw the way his stiff shaft strained and throbbed against his underwear and it made her shudder. The afterglow of the orgasm was coursing through her veins, but there was no relaxation as the erection that was going to make her a woman came in view. The thick head was partially covered by the foreskin, but she could see the glisten of pre-cum on slick skin. Her breath came out in ragged gasps as Thomas stripped completely naked. He was going to take her while she was strapped down and at his mercy, and she wondered if that was his ultimate fantasy about his patients.

She could do nothing but watch as he got on the table and knelt between her spread open thighs. He grabbed hold of his cock to stroke touches along it and she watched in fascination as the foreskin was dragged down off the angry-looking head. It was swollen red with hot blood and twitched as Thomas's slender fingers slid over it.

Jenny held her breath as he got over her on all fours and leaned down to a kiss. The passion flared even more as their lips remained together and she let out a muffled whimper as the weight of his body dropped down on her. She squirmed as the hardness of his erect length rubbed against her inner thigh, and when the kiss ended she didn't open her eyes.

"Look at me," he told her.

Jenny slowly opened her eyes and stared up at him. She was breathing heavily and their gazes remained locked together as he worked the tip of his cock right between her thighs until it was poised to enter her. The touch against her slick entrance made her gasp and her mouth remained open wide as she experienced the first full sex of her life. The burst of pleasure as her pussy lips were stretched open by a rampant cock made her groan, and she looked deep in Thomas's eyes as he plunged his full length into the soft tightness of her virgin cunt.

He seemed unable to contain his lust for her and immediately began to thrust his hips back and forward. Jenny felt the slight pain of her wrists and ankles straining against the leather bonds as she was used by her lover. The sweat from Thomas's brow dripped down on her as he quickened his pace to make her his. The thrusts quickly became more forceful and it was obvious he was struggling to hold back straight away. The thrill of playing out his medical perversions was too much for him to cope with and he crashed his body between her thighs as he lost control.

He clenched his buttocks to stave off the release for a final few seconds and continued throwing himself forward until the pressure boiled over. Jenny watched as his head rocked back and she heard the guttural moan that spilled from between his lips as his body convulsed. A powerful stream of cum erupted inside her to make her shudder, and she couldn't stop trembling as Thomas's weight pressed down on her. She could feel the strong jerks of his erection as the bursts of thick white continued to splash inside her and his convulsions continued until he eventually had nothing left to give.

He remained on top of her gasping for breath as the calm slowly returned to his body and his erection remained inside her until the power drained from it. He pushed himself up as if he was going to get off the table, but his lips came down on hers before he did it. Jenny responded to the fiery touch that pressed on her lips and the breath rasped from her when it ended.

She wasn't sure quite what to say and remained quiet as Thomas dropped down to the floor. He quickly dressed then moved around the table to release the straps and free her. The slight awkwardness was palpable as she got down and hurried to pick up her clothes. The warmth of his seed trickled down her thighs and she wiped it away as she put her panties back on. In seconds she was clothed again and moved to the door. She was unaware that Thomas was right behind her and only realized it when he stopped her from leaving. The kiss was passionate when she turned and it trapped her head against the door. She slowly opened her eyes when it ended to see his gaze on her.

"This needs to remain our secret," he warned her.

She understood what he meant and nodded her head.

"I promise I won't tell anyone," she said and when he stepped back, she opened the door to rush down the stairs.

Chapter 12

"I knew it, I bloody well knew it," Maggie exclaimed in a piercing voice. "You gave him his fantasy in his home."

"Stop talking so loud," Jenny whined and glanced around the entrance of The Teahouse. It was empty, but that didn't stop her worrying that someone might hear. "And anyway I didn't have a choice," she went on.

"Why not?" Maggie asked.

"Can we go somewhere more private?" Jenny replied. "My final words to him last night were that I wouldn't tell anyone, so you have to promise me this will stay between just us."

"OK, wait," Maggie said.

Less than a minute later, one of the girls was sitting at the table and complaining that she'd be making no money, but Maggie ignored her as she walked further inside the building. She led Jenny to the stairs then up to the first floor and they ended up in the room where the teenage girl's transformation was achieved not so long ago.

It seemed like an age to Jenny as she glanced around the room, and she threw herself down on a chair and leaned forward to put her head in her hands. Her hair spilled forward to hang down, and it was only when the older woman brushed it back that she looked up again.

"It can't be that bad," Maggie said.

"Are you kidding me?" Jenny exclaimed. "This is a complete disaster."

"So what happened exactly?" Maggie went on and sat down.

Jenny let out a sigh as she completed the job of sweeping her hair back from her face.

"It all went wrong," she said in a hushed voice.

"Well that doesn't tell me much," Maggie replied.

Jenny closed her eyes for a second, but it only brought her the image of Thomas Winterbourne's face and she quickly snapped them open again.

"When I left here after the last meeting, I wasn't really sure what I was going to do," she started then hesitated.

"And?" Maggie encouraged her.

"And... yesterday evening I decided to go through with the plan to steal the jewelry from Thomas's bedroom like Andy wanted me to," Jenny went on.

"But I thought you gave him..." Maggie started.

"He caught me," Jenny interrupted her.

"Oh..." Maggie let out and the word stretched out. "That's why you had no choice."

Jenny nodded her head.

"I panicked and needed to come up with something to get out of trouble," she said. "I thought he might bring in the police otherwise."

"So you offered him... you," Maggie let out in a hushed voice.

Jenny stared at the older woman but said nothing at first. She dropped her gaze to the floor and it was a few seconds before she started talking again.

"Yes," she admitted. "I told him the break in next door gave me the idea and it was a spur of the moment thing."

"He doesn't know that robbery really was you?" Maggie asked.

"It seemed like the sensible thing to do was lie and deny it when he asked," Jenny went on. "I made the offer that if he didn't bring the police into things, that I would let him use me however he liked in his examination room."

"How exactly did you explain that you know about his fantasies?" the older woman went on.

The flush of red stained Jenny's cheeks as she spoke.

"There was a patient in the house on Saturday," she said. "I… well I hid in the wardrobe in the examination room and got a glimpse of the treatment he gives."

"Really?" Maggie let out.

She'd been on the receiving end of one of Thomas's massages in the brothel, but she was interested in just what he got up to in the confines of his examination room with a real patient.

"Yes, I really did do it," Jenny confessed.

"What did he do?" Maggie asked.

"He gets his patient naked and massages the pressure points on their bodies to try and relax them," Jenny answered. "It is a medical procedure that apparently does help to cure the symptoms of female hysteria, but at the end of it I saw just how excited it made him."

"Did the patient see?" Maggie went on as her curiosity grew.

"No," Jenny told her. "He wears a loose white coat that covers his... well his..."

"Erection," Maggie finished the sentence.

"Yes," Jenny went on. "But I was hiding behind some boxes in the base of the wardrobe, so I saw it when he removed the coat after the patient left."

"No wonder he gets frustrated," Maggie mused almost to herself.

"Not any more," Jenny said and leaned forward to put her head in her hands again.

"You like him, don't you?" Maggie said.

The question startled Jenny and she was about to deny it when she looked up, but didn't get the chance.

"When you left after the last meeting, Andy commented it was likely the stress of the job that was getting to you," Maggie went on. "But I knew it was something more. You really do like him, don't you?"

Jenny closed her eyes as she nodded her head.

"Yes," she admitted. "I like him."

"So what happened to your hatred of the upper classes?" Maggie said.

"Does it matter?" Jenny let out in a despairing voice. "Whether I like him or not isn't the point." The legs of the chair scraped across the floor as she got to her feet. "It's not like anything can really happen between us anyway," she went on in a louder voice. "And more to the point, what the hell do I tell Andy?"

She turned to look at Maggie, but no response came back.

"He's expecting me to turn up with a fistful of jewelry," Jenny went on. "And now I'm in a position where I can't do that."

"Sit down," Maggie told her.

"I don't want to sit," Jenny replied and her distress was clear. "What am I going to do? Everything's gone wrong."

Maggie got up from where she was sitting and moved across the room to put her arm around the teenage girl's shoulder. She led her back to the chair and made her sit then dropped down next to her.

"What am I going to do, Maggie?" Jenny asked.

The older woman sighed.

"Look, the best thing you can do is return to the mansion," she said.

"But…" Jenny tried to interrupt.

"Don't argue," Maggie went on. "It will give me a chance to think about what you can do. Does Thomas know you left his home?"

"I told the butler I was going to see my aunt and he let me out," Jenny answered.

"Then go back," Maggie urged. "You don't want to leave anyway, do you?"

Jenny hesitated, but the last comment was the truth. The last thing she wanted to do was flee the mansion, but she wasn't sure where going back would get her.

"What about Andy?" she asked.

"If you're at the mansion then he's none the wiser that things have gone wrong," Maggie replied.

"But he will go mad if…." Jenny said.

"You let me worry about Andy Kent," Maggie interrupted.

"What are you going to do?" Jenny asked.

Maggie shrugged her shoulders.

"That's a good question," she replied. "I just need a day or two to think. Maybe I can come up with something."

It ended the conversation and Jenny followed the older woman out of the room and back down to the front entrance of the brothel. She turned back before she left and her voice was hushed when she spoke.

"He said I belonged to him now, but how can that happen?"

Maggie smiled as she reached out a hand to cradle the younger girl's cheek. She was aware of the twinge of jealousy, but she shrugged it off easily.

"Don't worry," she said. "Things will work out."

The words did little to comfort Jenny or lift the mood of despondency enveloping her. When she left the brothel and walked into the gloom of a cold evening, she could only imagine that when things did work out, it wouldn't be good for her.

Chapter 13

"Mr. Winterbourne has some work he needs done in his study," Stevens said.

"Can't Jill do it?" Jenny replied as she looked up from the bed she was tidying.

"He needed Jill to run out and buy some things for him," Stevens went on. "You're the only maid in the house just now, so finish what you are doing and go to the study."

"OK," she replied and waited until the elderly butler left the room before letting out a sigh.

It was now a couple of days since she walked out of The Teahouse brothel to return to the mansion and for all that time her mind had been in turmoil. She desperately wanted to be alone with Thomas again, but at the same time went out of her way to avoid that happening. Her emotions were constantly on edge and she veered from the thought of running away from everything to the idea of telling Thomas how much she wanted to be his. It was crazy and she was finding it difficult to cope more than ever.

She let out another sigh as she gathered her gear and walked out of the bedroom. There was always the chance that Thomas actually did want some cleaning work carried out, but Jenny suspected that was just wishful thinking as she made her way down the staircase to the lobby area. She walked along the hallway and tried to compose herself when she got to the study door. Lifting her hand, she knocked and waited.

"Enter," the voice from within shouted.

She took a slow breath and turned the knob to open the door so that she could walk inside. The smile on his face melted her heart right away, but it was the blossoming heat between her thighs that got her attention. She knew straight away that the encounter was going to be sexual and a shiver trickled down her spine. Her hand was shaking as she closed the door.

"Lock it," Thomas told her.

She remained where she was after doing it and just watched as he stood and moved around the desk. He arrowed straight towards her and she gasped as his kiss ravished her mouth.

"This isn't very secret," she said when it ended.

"I don't care," he replied and the hunger for her showed in his voice. "I couldn't wait any longer."

"I thought you were only interested in getting me in the examination room," Jenny commented.

"Oh... I want so much more than that," Thomas went on. "Didn't you understand it when I said you belong to me?"

"But how can we...." Jenny tried to say, but a soft fingertip pressed on her lips to stop her saying any more.

She closed her eyes as his hand caressed her cheek and knew that she wouldn't be able to resist. Just being close to Thomas was already making her lose control and she gasped as another kiss ravaged her lips.

"This is crazy," she said in a hushed voice when it ended.

"Don't you think I know that?" Thomas replied and turned away. "I've lived the last few years thinking there is something wrong with me because of my sexual fantasies about the patients I treat, but hoping at the same time that I would meet someone that shared them."

"And now you have," Jenny let out quietly.

Thomas turned back to her.

"And now I have," he said to echo her words. "I could tell the minute you offered yourself to me that it was about more than just using sex to get yourself out of trouble. I could see it in your eyes."

Jenny shuddered at the tight grip on her shoulders and tilted her face up for another kiss. Thomas pressed his body against her and she shivered at how hard he already was.

"Take me upstairs," she said when their lips parted.

"Not this time," Thomas replied.

"We can't do anything here," she said and gasped.

"The door is locked," he told her with a smirk. "Jill is out and Stevens and Matilda are down in the servants' quarters."

Jenny couldn't stop the rush of red-hot arousal that coursed through her veins and her legs began to tremble as Thomas's hand slid down from her shoulder to cup her breast. Her nipple stiffened immediately and she knew she was going to succumb.

"Let me pleasure you this time," she said.

Thomas stepped back and released his grip on her breast.

"I won't argue with that," he replied.

Jenny's nerves shot up. She made the offer and now wasn't quite sure how to carry through with it. A glance down showed Thomas's erection bulging against the front of his pants and she dropped to her knees before him to get a better look. His hand stroked on her hair as she reached out to press her palm against his crotch and the swell of breath made her shudder.

"So hard," she let out quietly.

"Get it out," Thomas ordered.

It appeared he wasn't about to let her have full control of the situation, but that suited her fine. His instructions would let her know what it was he wanted and she planned to give it to him. Her own hunger for what was happening came on stronger and she fumbled with the buttons of his pants to get them loosened. When the gap opened up, she slipped her hand through and worked it below his underwear. She almost squealed when her fingertips touched on hot, hard flesh. A glance up showed she was being watched and she slowly circled her fingers around Thomas's stiff shaft and eased it out through the gap.

Her fingers gripped tighter and she watched with wide open eyes as she rolled the foreskin down to expose the head completely. She heard Thomas's quiet groan and glanced up again. He seemed to be enjoying the touch of her fingers, so she gave him more by stroking them up and down. It was the sexiest of sensations to be turning a man on, and her seductress nature bubbled to the surface as she continued stroking.

"Use your mouth," Thomas ordered her.

Jenny slid her hand almost to the base of his cock and clung on as she obeyed him by leaning forward. The taste of his pre-cum spread on her lips as she kissed slick skin, and she flicked out her tongue to lick at it. The pressure on her head by Thomas's hand pushed her lower and she heard his gasping breaths as she opened her mouth to let his erection slide inside. Her pulse was racing as she slowly ducked her head down more and clamped her lips around his hardness. The feel of them sliding over veins bulging with hot blood was a turn on, and she bobbed her head to get more of it.

"Yes," Thomas groaned as his fingers gripped in her hair. "Keep doing that."

Jenny didn't want to stop as she enjoyed her first experience of pleasuring a man with her mouth. The thrill of it grew as she slid her touch up and down at a faster pace. Her excitement mounted as she carried on and it was Thomas that eventually ended things by pulling her head up. He got her to her feet and led her around the desk then dropped in his seat. Her eyes narrowed as he released his grip on her wrist and reached for the belt holding up his pants. The fear erupted that he was about to punish her again, and she turned her back to him nervously when he told her to.

Her breath came out in a rush as her hands were dragged behind her back and her wrists held together. The belt was looped around them and she grimaced as it was tightened. It seemed his fantasies of having a girl tied up extended past his examination table, and there was no resisting him when he helped her bend forward over his desk. She was completely at his mercy again and savoring every second of it. Her legs shook as the hem of her uniform was slowly hitched up the back off her thighs to reveal more and more naked skin until the material was around her waist. She pressed her face against the wood as Thomas stroked his fingertips across her panties.

"So pretty," he let out.

Jenny squirmed as his fingers slipped between her thighs and she knew there was no way he could miss the dampness already staining the material.

"I definitely found the right girl," he said.

Jenny bit her lip as his touch stroked along her pussy through the slick material. It was making her squirm around on the desk top and the burning rush of arousal grew stronger in her body. She held her breath as Thomas pulled his fingers from between her thighs to reach for the waistband of her panties. The white cotton was dragged halfway down her thighs and it exposed her rounded cheeks. The touch of fingertips caressing across her naked skin made her tense and she closed her eyes tightly as it slid along the crease of her ass.

It brought back memories of being on the examination table, when she was finger fucked and licked to an orgasm. She was expecting the same thing again but realized that Thomas was impatient for more when he got to his feet behind her. His hand touched on her lower back as he moved forward, and Jenny groaned as the hardness of his erection rubbed against her ass cheeks.

"You want it, don't you?" he said in a hoarse voice.

"Yes... yes," Jenny let out.

She groaned as he humped against her and forced his stiff shaft between her ass cheeks. The touch of it rubbing on her puckered skin brought out her shame but didn't stop her pushing back to get more. Thomas rocked his hips to stroke his cock more firmly between her naked cheeks and it was bringing out a side of her nature that she'd kept suppressed. The longing for more filled her mind and all she could think about was being his in that moment.

His hands gripped her hips as he moved back to give himself just enough room to slide his erection between her thighs from behind. The tip probed at her pussy lips until Thomas managed to slip it inside her tight entrance, and she gasped as he thrust forward to make her take every last inch. It trapped her in place on the desk and the growing tension made her wrists strain against the belt holding them together.

Thomas circled his hips to make his erection grind on her slick inner skin and there was no holding in the groan. The first sex they shared ended relatively quickly as he couldn't hold on at the end of his fantasy coming to life in the examination room. Jenny could sense that wasn't going to happen on this occasion and that her lover was in complete control of himself. She tensed as the grip on her hips tightened and the long, slow thrusts that fucked cock deep inside her pussy were delicious. There was going to be no frantic rush to an orgasm, but she was sure she was going to be taken all the way.

She writhed around on the desk top as the heat of arousal swelled between her thighs. Her tight pussy was stretched wide with every thrust and the sweat prickled on her forehead as the sensual, deep stroking of cock into her pussy continued. Thomas eased her back so that her thighs weren't trapped against the desk and his hand crept around her body to slide between her thighs. The touch on her clit brought out a shuddering groan and while fingers brushed back and forth over it, her lover pushed forward to hold his cock inside her. Jenny could feel the throb of hot flesh and her pussy pulsed around it as the touches on her clit set her body alight.

She was gasping for breath and shuddering when Thomas relented and pulled his fingers from between her thighs. He grabbed the belt with one hand to haul her arms back as he began to throw himself forward again. This time it was with more vigor and she could hear his heavier breathing as he increased his efforts to drive his swollen shaft between her slick pussy lips. His other hand trailed up her spine until his fingers slid in her dark hair and she winced as his grip tightened. It lifted her head up from the desk to make her gasp and the gentleness was gone.

Thomas's muscular midriff began to crash against her butt as his lust came out and he fucked his cock in her with increasingly powerful strokes. It was building her excitement towards a peak, and she tried to push herself back against him to meet his thrusts. The sex was spiraling out of control as their insatiable hunger for each other erupted and there was suddenly no holding back. Her lover was now going all out to fuck her to an orgasm, and the sweat rolled down her forehead as the erotic heat flared in her body. The feel of a thick, solid erection driving deep with a forceful passion was overwhelming and there was no restraining herself. The pressure built until she was at the breaking point and suddenly she was engulfed in the shudders of an intense orgasm.

She closed her mouth tightly to hold in the sound, but a muffled squeal came out as Thomas drove his erection deep and held it inside her. The pulsing of her slick inner skin around the throbbing hardness was uncontrollable and the spasms sent her climbing to a shattering high that took her breath. The climax still enveloped her body when the thrusts from behind started again and they quickly became frantic. Shudders wracked her petite frame as her lover joined her in losing control and his body slammed forward for a final time to trap her thighs against the desk as the first stream of hot cum erupted inside her.

Jenny was lost to the sensation as Thomas's seed flooded her pussy and she was given more and more as his body convulsed against her. His body arched to push his hips forward and he tried to fuck his cock deeper still as the last of the convulsions rocked him. He staggered back afterwards to drop in his seat when the power drained from his legs and he gasped for breath as he tried to recover his composure.

"Untie me," Jenny said. "Before someone comes and catches us."

"No one is going to…"

The words were ended by the knock on the door and Jenny gasped.

"Hurry," she let out in a panicked whisper.

Thomas was quick to untie the belt and Jenny pushed herself up from the desk then dragged her panties back in place. She turned to see him straightening his clothes and in a matter of seconds they were respectable again.

"Unlock the door and open it," he said quietly.

Jenny wiped the sweat from her forehead and combed her fingers through her hair as she walked across the room. She inhaled deeply a couple of times and glanced back to make sure Thomas was sitting at his desk before turning the key quietly in the lock and immediately opening the door. She backed off as Stevens walked inside.

"There's a lady here to see you, Mr. Winterbourne," the elderly butler said.

"I'm not expecting a patient to arrive," Thomas replied as a frown creased his brow.

"She isn't a patient, sir," Stevens went on. "But she insists that she knows you and that she has something of importance to discuss with you."

"Who is it?" Thomas asked.

"My name is Maggie Green."

Jenny's mouth dropped open as she watched the Madame of The Teahouse brothel walk in the room, and she turned to see that the expression on Thomas's face matched her own.

Chapter 14

The click of the door closing echoed in the stunned silence and Jenny glanced across the room to see that the elderly butler had made a diplomatic exit from the study.

"What the hell are you doing here, Maggie?" she let out as she brought her gaze back to the older woman.

"You know her?" Thomas said in a surprised voice as he looked back and forth between them.

"Yes, she knows me," Maggie replied. "In fact it's because of me that she's here."

Thomas opened his mouth as if he was going to say something more, but a confused expression crossed his face and nothing came out at first.

"I don't understand," he eventually managed to say.

"It's a long story," Maggie went on. "All I ask is that you give me the chance to tell it."

Thomas let out a sigh and stared at her as if he was considering her words. He finally indicated to the chair on the opposite side of the desk from him.

"Maggie," Jenny hissed through clenched teeth, "this is a bad idea."

"You might be right," the older woman agreed. "But considering all that has happened, he at least deserves to know the truth, and I think it may be the only way this will end well." She moved across to the seat and her gaze was on her feet when she dropped on it.

"So…?" Thomas urged her when she remained silent for a few seconds.

Maggie continued to stare at the floor as she considered how to start, but she eventually looked up.

"Do you remember being in The Teahouse when you let it slip to me that you were in need of a new maid?" Maggie asked him.

Thomas looked nervously at Jenny but brought his gaze back to Maggie as she continued talking.

"There's no need to worry about Jenny finding out anything about you. She already knows everything. Do you remember telling me about the maid?"

"Vaguely," Thomas admitted.

"Well, you also let slip that you used the Colwell Agency, and that put an idea in my head," Maggie went on.

"An idea?" Thomas repeated.

Maggie nodded her head as she stared across the desk at him.

"The manager of the Colwell Agency, Mr. Hollinger, is also a customer of The Teahouse," she told him. "So it gave me an opportunity to put some pressure on him with regard to the person that was supplied to your home."

Jenny was aware of Thomas's gaze coming to her, but she kept her eyes fixed firmly on the floor.

"So Jenny isn't a maid," he said.

"No," Maggie confirmed. "I'm sure she would be an excellent maid if she put her mind to it, but her particular talents lie elsewhere."

"As a thief," Thomas said.

"Yes," Maggie replied. "She is a professional thief that works for a man called Andy Kent. He likes to make out that he is a hardened boss of a criminal empire, but in truth it is mostly an act and there is a lot more to him than that."

"In what way?" Thomas asked.

"You have to understand his background first," Maggie went on. "Until ten yeas ago, he was an honest, hard working man that was no more remarkable than any other. He labored as a locksmith to look after his family, but everything he loved was taken from him one fateful night. No one really knows how the fire in his home started, but when he got there it was an inferno and he could hear the cries of his wife and children. He tried to get in to save them and still bears the burn mark on his palm where he desperately fought to open the door and get inside. It was impossible, though, and his family perished."

"That's terrible," Thomas interrupted her.

"It was," she agreed. "And he was a broken man when I first met him. But he came through it and turned his energies to something else. Maybe he just wanted a replacement family, who knows? But he set his mind to helping the orphans in our neighborhood."

"By turning them into criminals," Thomas commented.

Maggie shrugged her shoulders.

"He did what he thought was right to help get them off the street, as well as feed and clothe them," she went on. "It might seem wrong to someone from your background, but people can do desperate things in desperate times. Jenny is a classic example of the people he helped. She lost her mother at eight years old and was sent to an orphanage where beating the children was the way the well-to-do owners treated them. She ran away to live on the streets and it was Andy that got her off them and gave her a chance. He does that for a lot of kids, and it's not just the ones that work for him that he helps. There are a lot of single mothers and orphans in our east end neighborhood that have a much better life because of what he does. It might not be right in the eyes of the law, but nobody else makes the effort to help them."

"OK, I get what you're telling me," Thomas said. "He's a good man that was brought down by circumstances out of his control and is trying to make the best of things... but why are you telling me?"

"Andy and his gang do what they do because they have no choice," Maggie went on. "If there was an alternative for them, I'm sure they would take it."

"And that alternative would be me," Thomas said. "Or more to the point, the money I could provide."

"I hope so," Maggie replied. "What happened with Jenny arriving here was because of me. I applied some pressure on Mr. Hollinger to make sure a thief was introduced to your home and the intention was to steal from you and your neighbors."

"So it was you that robbed the house next door?" Thomas said as he turned his gaze to Jenny.

"Yes," she confessed.

"Can you get back what you stole?" he asked.

"No," Jenny replied. "It's already been sold on."

Thomas's lips tightened as he brought his attention back to Maggie.

"So why exactly should I help you after what you've done?" he asked.

"Because it will get you what you want," she went on and motioned her head to the pretty nineteen-year-old girl standing watching them. "I can't speak for Jenny, but I would suspect that if Andy needs to carry on with the life he leads just now, she would probably go back to help him. She owes him a lot and whatever you want to say about her, she's a loyal girl."

Thomas looked at Jenny.

"Is that true?" he asked and saw her somewhat reluctantly nod her head.

"He's been like a father to me," she said. "If he needs me, then I have to help him."

"I've watched you come to The Teahouse over the last few years," Maggie interrupted them. "And it's obvious that there is a sense of shame in you that you need to resort to a brothel to get the satisfaction you want. Well... maybe you have finally met a girl that can give you everything you want and need right here in your home."

Thomas slumped back in his chair and tried to make sense of the thoughts raging through his mind. It was too much information for him to cope with; he leaned forward again to put his head in his hands.

"We should leave you to think," Maggie said.

Thomas looked at her and just nodded his head. His gaze went to Jenny as she left the room and he saw her glance over her shoulder towards him. Their eyes locked for a brief instant before she walked out.

"I'll tell Stevens the meeting is over," Jenny said when she and Maggie got to the lobby area. "He can come and let you out."

"You're not coming?" the older woman asked.

Jenny shook her head.

"I want to stay," she answered.

Nothing more was said and they just hugged quickly before she made her way down the stairs. She stopped at the kitchen door to tell Stevens that the guest was ready to leave then immediately walked along to her bedroom to avoid any questions. She removed her uniform and lay down on the bed. It might very well be her last night there, and she wasn't sure how she would react if Thomas decided not to help. Considering the way they tricked him, she wouldn't be surprised if he didn't, but there was no way of knowing.

She dozed fitfully for the next few hours as the darkness surrounded her but was suddenly alert at the sound of the knock on the door. There was no way of knowing who it was, and she debated just ignoring it and pretending she was asleep. When the knock sounded again two more times in quick succession, she guessed that the person outside wasn't going to give up. Her suspicions were that Jill's curiosity about the evening's events got too much for her, and she prepared herself to answer the questions that would inevitably be thrown at her. Getting to her feet, she put on her uniform then walked across the room and inhaled a deep breath before opening the door.

"What are you doing down here?" she let out in a hushed voice as she found herself staring at Thomas.

"Couldn't stay away," he replied. "Can I come in?"

The rush of her pulse came on strongly as Jenny moved out of the way to let him step forward, and she closed the door when he was inside.

"How did you even know I was still here?" she said.

"If the roles were reversed, I wouldn't have left," he said. "We think alike."

"So, what do you want?" Jenny asked.

"I want you to take me to see Andy Kent," he replied.

"Now?" she let out in a surprised voice. "It's the middle of the night."

"Isn't that when thieves operate?" he asked.

Jenny was thankful for the darkness as the blush of red spread across her face.

"I'm sorry," she said. "I really didn't want to steal from you, but…"

The finger on her lips stopped her words.

"You said it before yourself," he let out. "It got me what I wanted."

Jenny moved her head back.

"But…" she persisted.

It was a kiss that stopped her words this time, and her pulse quickened even more.

"Just take me to see Andy Kent," Thomas told her when it ended.

Jenny let out a sigh.

"OK," she agreed and went to the small wardrobe to get her coat.

She was sure Thomas's mind was made up to help, but there was still one glaring problem that he seemed to be ignoring. It was what she'd tried and failed to say to him, but now there was no chance as he led the way out of the room and along the darkened hallway. They crept up the steps to the lobby then made their way to the front door.

The sense of trepidation swept over Jenny as they left the mansion and walked down to the gates. Thomas unlocked them so that they could step through to the street.

"We're going to walk?" she asked.

Thomas nodded his head as he spoke.

"You lead the way."

"You're sure you want to do this?" she asked him.

"No," he said with a rueful smile. "But get going."

The dark streets were empty as Jenny hurried through them. Her mind went over and over the situation as she moved from the salubrious surroundings of west end mansions back to the more familiar ground of east end tenements. Nothing was spoken as they continued on their way and she wondered where that night was going to lead her. She still couldn't imagine things ending well and on a few occasions considered just turning around and telling Thomas to go home. They were from different worlds that didn't really go together and nothing was going to change that.

"That's it," she said as she pointed to the tenement building in which the gang of thieves lived. "You realize that Andy is going to be mad that I brought you here."

"Just get me inside," he told her.

She nodded her head as she resumed walking and led Thomas inside the dim hallway and up to a door. It was a few seconds before the hatch slid open after she knocked.

"Queen Victoria lives here," Jenny said straight away. The door opened and she walked inside. "Is Andy here?"

"He's in his bed," the answer came back.

"Well, wake him up and tell him to meet me in his study," Jenny went on.

The girl nodded and closed the door before running along the hallway. Jenny led the way to the study and she and Thomas walked inside. She moved to the oil lamp on the desk and got it working. The dim glow gradually brightened just as the door opened.

"You finally did it," Andy said as he hurried inside the room. "How…"

His words came to an abrupt end as he realized there were two people waiting for him.

"I got caught, Andy," Jenny let out.

His eyes narrowed as he stared at the man he now knew was Thomas Winterbourne.

"Why the hell did you bring him here?" he said.

"You've got Maggie to thank for that," Jenny went on.

"Maggie…" Andy let out in a confused tone.

"I'm not here to cause you any problems, Mr. Kent," Thomas interrupted them. "In fact, it's quite the opposite that I want."

"What's going on, Jenny?" Andy asked.

"Just listen to him," she urged.

He seemed unsure of what to do as he stared at them, but eventually moved across to the desk and sat down somewhat reluctantly.

"The plan that you set in motion unraveled a few days ago when I caught Jenny trying to steal the jewelry from my bedroom," Thomas went on. "She offered me something in return for my silence on the matter and I accepted."

The flush of color spread across Jenny's face again. It was such a refined way of saying that he teased and toyed with her on his examination table before taking her virginity, but she suspected that what happened didn't exactly need to be spelled out to Andy for him to understand the implications of what was being said. He glanced at her and she couldn't meet his gaze.

"OK," he said. "The two of you have an arrangement. What's that got to do with me and why are you here?"

"That would be because Maggie Green came to my home tonight," Thomas told him.

"And said what?" Andy asked.

"She made it clear to me what you did for Jenny and how much you mean to her," Thomas answered. "And that your protégé is unlikely to stop helping you… unless I offer you something."

The suspicious expression crossed Andy's face and he glanced at Jenny before returning his gaze to the other man in the room.

"What exactly is it that you can offer me?" he said.

"Help," Thomas replied.

"What sort of help would a man of your standing give me?" Andy went on and the suspicion was there in his voice.

"How many people do you control here?" Thomas asked.

"Why do you want to know that?" Andy countered.

"The gang is usually around ten to fifteen strong," Jenny answered the question.

She saw the look Andy flashed at her but ignored it.

"And how many around the neighborhood are the beneficiaries of your generosity?" Thomas asked next.

Andy knew that his silence would only result in Jenny answering the question, so he spoke straight away.

"It can vary depending on who's in need, but I guess it must be in the region of between thirty and fifty people at times."

"And you make enough to do that?" Thomas went on.

"Not always, but mostly we do," Andy replied.

"How much money does it take?" Thomas queried.

"We can get through ten pounds a month easily," Andy answered.

"OK," Thomas mused and hesitated for a second or two to think before carrying on. "So, if I supplied you with a sum of fifteen pounds a month that would mean you could continue your generosity, but with the stipulation that the kids in your care get an education in something other than thieving and robbery?"

"Why the hell would you do that?" Andy let out in a surprised tone.

"You have something special that is just as important to me now," Thomas said and the two men looked at Jenny.

She finally voiced the fears that had been building up in her mind over the last few days.

"But how can we be together?" she said. "You're a wealthy, upper class doctor with a reputation to maintain, and I'm just a common thief. How exactly…"

"You're certainly a thief," Andy interrupted her. "No question about that, but you might not be as common as you think."

Jenny's face scrunched up as she frowned.

"What do you mean I might not be so common?" she asked in a hushed voice.

"Your mother was a beautiful woman," Andy went on.

"You didn't know her," Jenny countered.

"No, you're right, I didn't," Andy replied. "But the rumors about her were that she was beautiful."

"What rumors?" Jenny snapped.

"You might want to sit down," Andy told her.

"No, I'll stand," she said. "What rumors?"

"What did your mother tell you about your father?" Andy asked.

"Nothing," Jenny answered. "I asked, but she wouldn't tell me anything about him."

"I think I know why that was," Andy went on. "It wasn't something I knew when I first got you off the streets, but you let slip once that her name was Chloe Marks and I decided to do some checking."

"I thought your surname was Green," Thomas said to Jenny.

"That was only for this job," Andy replied. "Her real name is Jenny Marks. What I found out was only speculation, and I couldn't confirm it, but the people I spoke to informed me that your mother's beauty caught the attention of a young Lord. It led to an affair that burned brightly but was over quickly. The story I heard was that his parents found out and were less than impressed by his choice of girl, so they sent him overseas. It wasn't before your mother fell pregnant with you, though, and she used the name Marks to give you something from your father."

"I don't believe it," Jenny let out. "Why wouldn't she tell me that and, more to the point, why the hell didn't you tell me?"

"I didn't find out until you were in your teens," Andy told her. "Your hatred of the upper classes was obvious by then, so I didn't think you would exactly welcome the news. I decided it would be better just to let sleeping dogs lie and leave you ignorant of the fact that you might have blue blood running in your veins. Why your mother didn't tell you, I have no idea. Maybe she was scared you would try to find him or maybe that he would take you away from her if he found out."

Jenny moved across to the seat on the opposite side of the desk from Andy and slumped down on it. A night of revelations starting with Maggie's appearance at the mansion was ending with her getting the biggest shock of all. She flinched at the touch on her shoulder and looked up to see Thomas staring down at her.

"Maybe it's time for us to go home, Lady Marks," he said with a smile.

"That's not funny," she complained.

"But it might be true," he replied. "Maybe you can help give the upper classes a better reputation."

"It might be completely wrong and nothing but a false rumor," she went on. "I might simply be Jenny Marks, professional thief."

"Go with him, Jenny," Andy encouraged her.

"You just want me to go so you can get the money," she said.

"Yeah, that's true," he replied with a grin. "But a father, even a surrogate father, knows what's best for his child. You should go with him."

She got to her feet in a daze and didn't protest when her hand was taken to lead her out of the study and along to the front door.

"I'll speak to you soon," Thomas said to Andy.

The older man nodded his head and opened the door to let them leave. Jenny just followed as they walked out into the darkness of the night. She barely said a word when they started walking home as she tried to digest the news she just heard. Thomas hailed a Hansom cab when it passed by and it got them back to the mansion quicker. They quietly let themselves through the large gates then into the property.

When the door was closed, Jenny automatically walked in the direction of the stairs leading down to the servants' quarters. The grip on her hand tightened to stop her and she looked at Thomas.

"Where are you going?" he asked.

"I'm going to bed," Jenny replied.

"Not down there, you aren't," he went on.

"Wait… I can't," she protested.

Thomas was much too powerful for her to resist and she was taken to the stairs leading to the first floor and led up them. In a matter of seconds, she was walking inside his bedroom. The tiredness faded as memories of her last time in the room flooded her mind. What began as a robbery ended with her tied down to an examination table and being used. Her pulse raced as she yanked her hand free and moved across the room to the box on the dressing table.

"Just can't help yourself, can you?" Thomas said with a grin.

"Do you think your grandmother would mind?" she asked him when she opened the box to take out the pearls.

"No," he replied. "Before she passed away, she told me to find someone beautiful to wear them."

Jenny smirked as she placed the string of pearls around her neck and secured them in place. Even after all that happened that night, her excitement welled up at being alone with Thomas and she couldn't stop herself.

"Beautiful enough?" she teased him.

"Hmm... I'm not sure about the coat and uniform," he said.

Jenny's heartbeat quickened as she removed the coat then dragged the uniform over her head and dropped it on the floor. It left her standing in just her panties and bra and she lifted the pearls and teased them on her lips.

"Is that better?" she asked.

She could see the effect the coquettish look was already having on him, and heavy breathing made her chest rise and fall noticeably as he closed the distance between them.

"You know what we're doing is madness, don't you?" Jenny said when he was standing right in front of her.

"Yes," he replied. "Do you want to leave?"

She slowly shook her head as she looked up at him. His closeness was enough to bring out her own arousal and when he lifted his hand to touch the pearls, she nuzzled and kissed his fingertips. His gentle touch brushing across her lips was making her want more and she let the necklace drop down. Thomas leaned in to kiss her and she gave up worrying what was going to happen between them. That was for the future and she just wanted to live in the here and now.

His hand caressed against her cheek and she moved forward to make his growing erection press on her midriff. The thrill of bringing her lover fully erect wasn't lost on her and she could feel the passion coming through in his kiss. The excitement of being wanted so badly made her shudder and she let out a gasp when their lips parted. Thomas grabbed her wrist to drag her over to the bed and her gasp was louder as he pushed her down onto it.

She scrambled to move up towards the pillows and watched as he took off his jacket and shirt. In an instant his pants were on the floor too and she froze as he got on all fours on the bed and crawled over her. His head came down and the hunger for her came through even more in the kiss. Jenny lifted a hand to grope his erection through his underwear and heard his groan when their lips parted.

"I'm not so sure I'll measure up as a lady," she said with a grin.

"I don't want a lady in the bedroom," he replied.

She started to release her grip on his stiff shaft, but his hand came over hers to make her continue groping him.

"Don't stop," he urged her as he leaned down to nuzzle her neck.

Jenny gave him more by sliding her hand below his underwear to wrap her fingers around his erection. Her head pressed back against the mattress to stretch her neck out as soft kisses played on her skin. The sweet sensation sent shivers racing down her spine that she was unable to stop, and they got stronger as Thomas worked his lips lower on her body. His tongue slid along the top edge of her bra before he reached out a hand to ease the material lower. It exposed a nipple and he fell on it hungrily.

Jenny's grip tightened around his cock as her nipple was sucked erect. The bra was dragged down to reveal more and she groaned as every inch of her soft curves were explored by an eager mouth. It brought out the wetness between her thighs and she could feel the pulsing throb of Thomas's erection as hot blood flowed. She needed to let go as he kissed further down her body, and it brought her the anticipation of a touch in her most intimate spot.

Thomas's mouth grazed across her panties to make her arch up and she spread her legs for him. Her underwear was dragged down to her ankles to be taken off and she rolled over on her belly.

"Unhook my bra," she said.

It was quickly done and when she turned onto her back again, she was wearing nothing more than a necklace. Her fingers brushed across the smooth, rounded pearls as she spread her legs to give her lover what he wanted. He leaned down to kiss on her inner thigh and the touch of his tongue licking a wet trail higher made her close her eyes tightly as the anticipation rose in her mind again. There were no panties in the way now and she groaned as soft kisses pressed on her slick, naked skin.

Her taste was what Thomas wanted and his tongue came out to get more of it. Her back arched as fingertips slid between her thighs to spread her swollen lips open. Jenny gasped as her lover's tongue swept across her pink, glistening skin. The shivers of delight were uncontrollable and the surge of exhilaration brought out her longing for the touches.

She reached down to slide her fingers in Thomas's unruly red hair as his tongue slipped deeper inside her. Her butt lifted up from the mattress and her grip tightened as the touch inside her inner depths made her muscles tense and flex. She was being taken on a ride to an orgasm and the flames were burning hotter between her thighs as she got closer to it.

The touches ended before she got there, and she tried to hold on to Thomas's hair to keep him between her thighs. He wanted more and knocked her hand away as he moved to lie beside her and dragged his underwear down. Jenny shuddered as she was rolled onto her side and the touch of a muscular body pressed against her back.

The hardness of a solid erection played against her naked butt and she let out a long gasp when a hand came around her body to find her breast. A soft caress turned to a rougher grope as Thomas dug his fingers in her soft flesh. It lit up her desire even more and she squirmed as he worked his erection between her thighs. It played against her slick entrance for only a brief instant before sliding in to spread her pussy open. She was held in a tight embrace as every last inch was fucked inside her.

Thomas nuzzled his mouth against the nape of her neck and she was lost to the moment as he began to gently rock his hips. The movement stroked his cock in and out of her pussy as kisses ravaged her sensitive skin. Her breasts were still being groped and her body was alive with blossoming sensations that were driving her towards a high. Hard muscles rubbed against her back as she was held in an even tighter embrace, and she reveled in the close connection with a man that wanted her so passionately. She expected the sex to become rougher as his lust erupted, but let out a groan when his erection pulled out.

Thomas's hands gripped her hips to make her roll onto on her back and she looked up at him when he got over her. His lips brushed against hers when he leaned down, but the kiss gradually became more intense. Before it ended, he dropped down so that his erection was back between her thighs. She looked in his eyes when he lifted his head and knew that the sex wouldn't stop this time until they were both exhausted. Their gazes remained locked together as he entered her and Jenny's mouth opened wide as the hard thrust buried the full length of his cock inside her. She closed her eyes as he leaned down, but the expected kiss didn't come. Instead, his lips brushed softly across her cheek until his breath was warming her ear.

"I love you," he whispered.

The words startled her and she opened her eyes. It was what she was feeling, but she never expected to hear it.

"I love you too," she replied as she wrapped her arms around his body and pulled him down on top of her.

The connection felt even closer as they held in the embrace and the passion flared. Thomas pushed himself up and she stared at him as he began to thrust his hips. The lick of hot flames played between her thighs again as his erection plunged inside her, and in seconds they were both gasping for breath. Jenny slid her hands to his lower back and urged him on to more as he threw himself forward with relentless effort to give them both the pleasure they wanted.

It wasn't long before the fire began to burn out of control, and she could feel the growing tension in her body as she was fucked to the very cusp of a climax. She instinctively dug her nails in Thomas's back and it made his hips drive forward to slam his stiff shaft inside her. The sound of their naked skin slapping together filled the room until it was too much for Jenny and the pressure released. Crashing shudders overwhelmed her body as she surrendered herself to the ecstasy and she writhed around under her lover as he continued to fuck her.

She was still climbing the heights of her passion when Thomas succumbed to the excitement and she moaned as his cock quivered inside her before erupting to life. He dropped down and pressed his face against her neck as the strong spurts of cum made his body convulse. They were held in the moment as the sex played out to an end before the shudders turned to trembling as some semblance of calm returned to their bodies.

Jenny could feel the fading throbs of Thomas's erection as her pussy continued to spasm around it, but the sensation eventually ended to leave them locked together in an embrace.

"You didn't tie me up this time," Jenny couldn't help teasing him when he rolled to the side and lay beside her.

"I'll save that for the leather table upstairs," he shot back.

Jenny shook her head and laughed, but she knew that she likely would be enticed back to the examination room. Her laughter was quick to end, though, as she moved to rest her head on Thomas's chest and cuddled close to him.

"What are we really going to do now?" she asked.

"We take each day as it comes and see where it gets us," Thomas replied.

It was as good an answer as she was going to get. There was no knowing what would happen tomorrow or the days following that, but she knew she was where she wanted to be and that her life as a professional thief was over.

"I can live with that," she murmured and closed her eyes to listen to the sound of a slowing heartbeat.

Epilogue

"So she was a naughty girl then, Granpa Andy?" Chloe said and giggled.

"Oh yes, very naughty," Andy replied as he looked down at the pretty five-year-old girl sitting on his knee. "I had to tell her off all the time. She wasn't a good girl like you."

"I'm listening to this," Jenny said as she walked in the room.

"What?" Andy protested. "I'm telling the truth about you."

"Yes, well remember just who it was that taught me to be naughty," Jenny said.

"Granpa Andy," Chloe shouted.

"Yes, it was," Jenny told her daughter. "So don't you listen to anything he tells you. It's time for bed now, so say goodnight and get up the stairs. I'll send your father up to read you a story."

Chloe leaned in to kiss Andy on the cheek.

"You will tell me more, won't you?" she whispered.

Andy smiled and nodded his head before helping her jump down to the floor. He watched as she ran out the door of the lounge to do as she was told and go up to her bedroom.

"I think it's time for you and your stories to go home, Granpa Andy," Jenny teased him.

"I need to find my wife first," he said as he got to his feet.

"I know where she is," Jenny said.

She linked arms with him and they walked out towards the lobby area of the mansion then on towards the door. Maggie was standing chatting with Thomas at the front of the mansion and the pair of them turned at the sound of approaching footsteps.

"I'm getting thrown out," Andy joked.

"It's your own fault for telling tales to Chloe," Jenny said.

She released her grip on Andy's arm and he walked across to Maggie.

"Come on," he said. "We better go home and make sure that our orphans are in bed before they ruin the house."

Jenny watched as Thomas led the way down to the gate and opened it for the married couple to walk back towards their tenement home.

"I told our daughter that I would send you up to read her a story," Jenny told Thomas when he got back to her. "So get going before she starts shouting."

"Yes Miss," he replied.

He leaned in to kiss her before extinguishing the cigar in his hand and walking inside the house. Jenny looked around the tidy gardens on either side of the driveway before following her husband inside. She looked down at the Winterbourne family crest on the floor then walked across to where the Marks coat of arms was displayed. It was one of the few additions to the house after her marriage to Thomas.

"Blue blood in my veins," she murmured as she walked back towards the lounge to relax. "Who would have thought it?"

The End

Click HERE to sign up for Lolita London's mailing list.

http://mlgn.to/1okz

Your information is kept 100% private and never shared with anyone.

To request to join Lolita London's ARC team and receive FREE copies of her books before they're published in exchange for an honest review, enter your name and email HERE.

http://goo.gl/forms/RaUfwsUYnD

Manufactured by Amazon.ca
Bolton, ON